Once Blue

By
Ann Eastman Young

ISBN 978-0-557-71193-2

For My Mother

"Just as my fingers on these keys
Make music,
So these self-same sounds
On my spirit make music, too.

Music is a feeling then, not sound:
And thus is what I feel
Here in this room, desiring you,
Thinking of your blue-shadowed silk,
Is music."

- Wallace Stevens

Cover Art by Marion Eastman Blodgett
Editorial Assistance, Peter Keeley

CHAPTER ONE

June 1980

The first time I saw Blue, he was playing his guitar in the *Ripe Apple*. The place was hot that night and so was he. His fingers rode the strings of that guitar until they sang and glinted; Blue made those strings seem to sweat sparks. I could see right away there was something special about him. Man, he was good.

I wasn't supposed to be in the *Apple* that night. I was underage for one thing, and Rusty's only little sister besides. If he caught me there he'd drag me out by my ear, or worse. Rusty and his friends hung out at the *Apple* a lot, and I was just praying I wouldn't get caught. But Russell (nick-named Rusty) was always talking about this guy Blue around the house, saying what an incredible guitar player he was and how all the guys admired him. When he wasn't playing, though, Rusty said Blue was like a quiet bomb ticking, just waiting to go off. I decided I had to see for myself.

So I stood to the back and kept an eye on the table where Rusty and his friends were sitting. Blue had them all under his spell. It wasn't often the crowd in the *Apple* wasn't rowdy and carrying on. Surfers, bikers and locals hung out there every Thursday, Friday and Saturday night -- not exactly a quiet bunch. But that muggy night in June, they sat listening, hardly even sipping at their mugs of beer going warm. The summer really began for me that night. School was out, and somehow I knew that I was going to meet this Blue, and that nothing would quite be the same for me after.

The spotlight bathed him in gold, and his loose blond curls shimmered every time he moved. He stood a lean five-nine-or-ten. I could see the nice curves of his biceps working below his blue tee-shirt sleeves as he played, and taut thighs under his faded jeans. His eyes were closed, and his face tilted back in an expression I can only describe as rapture. I liked the clean sharp planes of his face: high cheekbones, strong chin, and straight nose.

But as I watched, I could see there was something simmering under the surface, just like Rusty said. You could almost feel heat coming off him, with something dark underneath. And all of it, the hidden dark and his surface gold fused into an arc of notes that spewed out like colored sparks from his electric guitar.

He was teaching those strings to talk and sigh and moan. The guitar's voice and his were one, the guitar an extension of his arms, his body. There was something naked about his playing, something raw. He was in the middle of a solo now, clearly improvising, and it gave me chills it was so bluesy, sweet and deep. He shared the stage with another guy who played rhythm guitar, a dark-haired bearded guy I recognized as one of Rusty's friends. But I hardly looked at him with Blue up there. He was riveting. His whole body cajoling that guitar-speak, his eyes squinted tight, pulling it out from the inside.

He started slow, the notes crying, drawn out long, then he built it up, faster and stronger until you couldn't stand it anymore—and he let it down fast. He launched into the last verse in his sweet-yet sandy-edged tenor and slid into the soaring chorus. Finally, the last chord rang out, lingered in the dark, and the place fell silent.

It must have been seventy-five degrees in that room, but I stood shivering, his music's echo hanging like silver shimmers after a white firework. Then the guys, Rusty and his friends, came to and started whistling, hollering and clapping

The dark-haired guy set his guitar down and wandered off the stage. I kept my eyes on Blue. He unplugged, wiped a cloth over his black electric guitar, and set it down on a metal stand. He moved slow, kind of dreamlike, still under the music's spell. He turned, smiled a sleepy smile, and waded off the stage through the crowd toward Rusty and the rest of the guys.

I could see that the closer he got to the table, the more he shook it off. With each step, he seemed to wake from the spell a little more. His magic dissipated, and he settled back down to earth. Finally he was at the table, and the guys thumped him on the back and handed him an icy mug of beer. He chugged down a few swallows and became one of them. But if my instincts were right, Blue was only himself when he was up there playing. The person he became with the guys was a kind of clever camouflage to hide behind. The truth of who he was lived up there, inside his music.

Reluctantly, I decided I better get out of there before Rusty or one of his friends stumbled into me. I was about to leave when a couple of girls I knew sashayed over to the guys' table and my heart sank stone-heavy to my stomach.

One of the girls was Patti, a girl Russell used to date. She was seventeen, with long wavy black hair, a great body and not much upstairs. But she looked just fine, and Patti liked "hot property." Whatever was in was okay with her, and Blue was obviously hot. She wanted him, I could tell.

2

The other girl with Patti was Joanie, big eyes, short blonde hair and "a little on the tough side," as my Mom would say. I wasn't worried about Joanie. She went out with a guy called Tucker. They were on and off, but mostly on. Joe Tucker was big and had been known to get nasty if anyone messed with Joanie. I figured Blue had more sense than that.

Patti was making big eyes at all of them, but especially at Blue. She was laying it on thick, talking loud, swaying her body in close, brushing accidentally-on-purpose against him, gesturing with her long, thin hands. Blue was flirting and smiling right back. Watching it made my stomach queasy, so I booked it out of there.

Outside I sucked in a few deep, smoke-free breaths. Mixed with the humid air, I caught the heady scent of a night-blooming jasmine somewhere nearby, my favorite. Florida nights were filled with good smells, especially in summer: the pungent breeze off the Gulf, whiffs of bougainvillea, gardenia, thick jungle smells-- flowers grew like crazy in dank, humid earth. You could almost feel things growing up through the dirt in fast motion. Spanish moss draped the live oaks in webs of green lace, and cicadas droned endlessly from the trees. I walked away from the *Apple* different from when I went in, with Blue's music weaving a gold thread through my mind.

I walked the mile home slowly. We moved to Florida from New Hampshire nine years ago. I was only seven then, but sometimes I still missed the variety of trees, the hills and mountains there, and snow at Christmas time. But Florida had grown on me. Summer nights on the Gulf seemed to be alive and breathing. The palm fronds whisked together in the breeze, rustling like whispered promises. The slow-fading sunsets and deep azure of the night sky beckoned you, called softly, making you feel restless and a little wild.

I wished I had time for a walk on beach, but I knew my mom would be getting worried. She didn't mind if I went out in the summer, as long she knew where I was and that I was home by ten or ten-thirty. It was getting close to that, and I knew I would hear about it if I was late. It was a drag having curfews, but my Mom was a single parent. She just didn't realize that sixteen wasn't as young as it used to be. Good or bad, my friends and I knew a lot already.

At the house I saw a light on in the living room, which meant Mom was still up. I told myself to calm down, no problem, I hadn't been drinking or anything.

But when Mom asked where I had been, I lied and said walking on the beach with my friend Sally. Sally would go along with the story if asked, we agreed on that earlier. I could tell Mom didn't really believe me, but she didn't want to come out and accuse me of lying. After watching television with me for awhile, she finally said she was tired, sighed, and promised we would *have to talk* in the morning. She kissed the top of my head and went up to bed.

I sat half-watching a dumb science fiction movie for awhile, with giant ants running amuck, but mostly I was thinking about Blue. I didn't like lying to my mother. I had been known to have a beer at a party now and then, but I hated being out of control. That kind of excess didn't interest me. I guess I was too wary for that, and I had seen enough friends' lives messed up from drinking or drugs. But my being at the *Apple* would have flipped her out. Sometimes I wondered if honesty truly was the best policy, like the saying claimed. When your father was dead, you just kind of protected your mother from certain things. Sure, I was stubborn and hard to handle sometimes, but I wasn't doing anything really *bad*. I didn't want to worry her for nothing. I finally gave up on the movie and went to brush my teeth.

While I was in the bathroom, I studied my face hard in the mirror, wondering if it was a face that would interest a guy like Blue. My eyes were my best feature, big and an unusual aquamarine color, with dark lashes. People had commented all my life on my eyes, so I figured they had to be all right. My nose was kind of a pointy, not so hot, with a small mouth. My lips were kind of nice though, full and red., with a small chin, heart-shaped face. Curly gold-brown hair: real curly, too wild and wind blown most of the time; I kept it on the short side. My mom's idea of a joke was always asking me why I couldn't find my hairbrush when she knew I hadn't lost it. But all in all, it was a face with something other than exotic beauty, which was what I longed for. Cute, maybe, attractive, yeah--- but beautiful, I was afraid not. At least I had a nice shape, though only five-foot three, I had an athletic, lean build.

I wondered if Blue was the kind of guy who appreciated cute. He struck me more as the type who went for Patti's kind of pretty and that worried me. I got into bed and finally dozed off with Blue's voice and his guitar playing his silver sparks of notes in my head. The way he moved, the way he looked, those slender fingers gliding across the strings of that guitar. I realized I had been looking for him all my life, without knowing it... Somehow I had been waiting to hear just that voice... his voice. As if I had heard it before somewhere, and part of me had been waiting, all my life, just to hear it again.

CHAPTER TWO

My brother Russell ran a motorcycle shop called *Hannan's Wheels*. He worked on "bikes" practically in his sleep, and that was why his business did so well. When he was in high school, he used to race all over the state of Florida, and he won lots of trophies and awards as a dirt rider. He had been taking motorcycles apart and putting them back together since he was twelve.

Mom wanted him to go to college, but Russ just wasn't the type. Like I said, Rusty was real smart in his own way, but he liked to make his own rules. School didn't agree with him. He played football and he was good, he probably could have gotten a scholarship to college somewhere. But I don't know, I think Rusty was genuinely happy running the shop. He helped Mom with finances and with Dad's insurance money, we had enough to get by. We did okay, the three of us. But Dad's dying hit Rusty hardest of all, I think. He was twenty-one now, but he was fifteen when it happened. It changed him a lot. But then, it changed everything.

Rusty was with the jock crowd before Dad died. I think he even would have gone to college for Dad's sake. He got good grades too. When Dad had his first heart attack, we all thought he'd get better. At least Mom and I did. But Rusty, right away, he started acting different.

Seeing Dad in the hospital afterwards - his face gray and pinched - hooked up to all these machines, with tubes up his nose, tubes making black and yellow marks up and down his arms - devastated Rusty. Dad had never looked weak any day in his life before that I could remember, and Russ didn't know what to do. My dad was a strong, vibrant guy his whole life, and then, Bam, the heart attack seemed to hollow him out, steal his light away. Rusty got quiet around us, but you could almost feel the anger radiating off his skin, like a fever.

Russell started hanging out with different guys then, getting in trouble, drinking and skipping school, and he started going by his nickname, Rusty. Mom was so preoccupied with her own sadness that she couldn't really deal with Russell carrying on, too. So she kind of ignored it in a way she would not have before. I think she figured Dad would handle it when he got better

But Dad never got better. He was in the hospital for three weeks. They kept saying he was improving, maybe he could go home soon, but instead he got grayer and quieter, his strong white light slowly seeping out of him. It made us all crazy to do nothing but stand there, day after day, watching him slip farther and farther downstream, not knowing why, or how to save him. The doctors tried a bunch of different things, but nothing seemed to work. They couldn't understand it. Finally, Mom came to get me at school one day.

I was called to the office from math class. I still remembered the walk down the dark hall. Time seemed stretched out, dream-like, and it took me forever to get to the end of it. I knew before they told me that Dad had died, of his second heart attack. He was forty-seven. It was weird how life went along pretty smooth, with minor problems, day-to-day stuff, nothing big. Then one day, one word, and suddenly, your whole life changed. I was ten when he died, but I still remembered the way his belly curved into me when he hugged me, his cigarette smoke-and-sawdust smell when he came home from work, and the way he would come into my room at night and brush my hair back from my face for a long time, soothing me to sleep. He was a supervisor for a large construction company called Conco. I remembered the way his hands held a cigarette, how his blue eyes crinkled in the corners when he smiled, and the hard, down-turned line of his mouth when he was mad. The way he propped his elbow out the open window of his truck, so he got a darker tan on one arm. I remember him tossing a baseball with me. He could make me laugh like no one else. I can't remember the sound of his laugh very well now, though I try and try to hear it, to call it back into my mind. I keep searching for the exact sound of it, but I can't get it back, not completely. It's funny, the things you remember about someone; they're not always the things you expect you would miss most. But you hold tight to them, because they're all you have left.

My mom got a job afterwards, as a receptionist in a dentist's office. She liked Dr. Simon (we'd been going to him for years) and she was good at talking to people and putting them at ease. In the past year, she had been getting trained as a hygienist, too. But when she got home, away from the bustle of her courses and the office, there was a sadness that still owned her, a distance I just couldn't reach through. We were close, closer than most mothers and daughters I knew, but there was still something far away about her since Dad died. She was still pretty at forty-six, and I wished she would find someone, maybe start dating. I didn't want her to be alone. But they wouldn't be Dad, and that was the problem. His ghost still owned her heart.

The morning after seeing Blue for the first time, I woke up with a smile on my lips. It occurred to me there was a chance that he hung out at Rusty's shop on Saturday mornings, like a lot of Rusty's other friends. It was kind of a pit stop for the guys on the way to surfing or the beach. I wondered if I might casually drop by, see who was there. Besides, I love getting motorcycle rides.

I kept begging Rusty to teach me how to drive one myself, and he said he would, but he kept putting me off until "later"-- which never came. I think the idea of me on a bike alone scared him. He probably figured I would drive like a maniac. He knew I was pretty fearless. I loved the freedom of it, air touching you all around, the sheer thrill. No walls or metal between you and the sights, smells, and sounds zipping by. You felt more on a motorcycle. True, it was dangerous and if you hit the asphalt with no protection, well, motorcycle accidents were the worst. But when my Dad died, I realized anyone could die, anytime at all. It made me less afraid. Living was the hard part, I figured, and I didn't want to miss anything. Besides, riding on a motorcycle was the sweetest rush I knew.

My mom hated motorcycles, for obvious reasons. I didn't know too many parents who did like them. Rusty and I were considerate, though; he didn't come barreling in the driveway screeching to a stop or anything. He took it slow, and Mom didn't know how often I got rides on the back. We didn't lie about it; we just kind of played it down a little. But a ride on the back of bike with Blue driving, now that would be something, truly something.

I could tell it was going to be another scorcher. Living in Florida, the heat was a fact of life. But the summer months could be brutal. The heat grew fat, like a giant dog standing over you, panting hot breath on you all day. I'd get out of the shower and be dripping sweat only an hour later. By the end of the summer, it even got too hot for the beach. The sand became impossible to walk on, it seared your feet, and the Gulf got so warm, it didn't cool you at all. But one good thing was that you hardly had to wear any clothes from May until October. I got up, took a quick shower and dressed carefully, on the off chance I might run into Blue.

Since I planned to hit the beach later, I decided to wear my turquoise bikini under my favorite jean cut-offs and a pale pink halter-top, cut just above my belly button. My stomach was already pretty tan, even though I had only been out of school two weeks. I put my sandals on-- the ones with white beads strung across the thin leather straps above my toes -- a sexy touch, I thought. I dreaded going down to face my mother. I had not forgotten she said we *had to talk*.

7

I grabbed a glass of V-8 and a piece of cinnamon bread from the fridge and strolled out to the lanai to eat. I knew Mom was around somewhere. She was always up early, even on Saturdays. She did the laundry or went grocery shopping or studied for her classes. She took ceramic classes one night a week and some Saturday mornings she would go to the community college to work on her pottery. I said hello to our cockatiel, Skipper, hanging in his white cage from the ceiling. He murmured, "L'o, L'o," back and rustled his silky white wings. He leaned his head down and I scratched the back of his neck through the wires of the cage.

I finished my juice and decided to go out to pick a grapefruit. There were orange and grapefruit trees right in our backyard, even an avocado tree. When we first moved to Florida, I couldn't get over being able to walk across dew-wet grass in bare feet, pluck a grapefruit or an orange, and eat it fresh from the tree. Like being on some tropical island. In New Hampshire we had apple trees, but that wasn't the same.

The birds, palmetto rats and the fruit flies loved the fruit too, though, so I checked them over for holes and rotten spots before I brought them in. I ate so many oranges my first year in Florida, I couldn't eat any at all for the year afterward. I took two grapefruit and two oranges into the kitchen to wash and found Mom pouring herself some coffee. I offered her an orange or a grapefruit. She chose an orange, and we took our fruit to the lanai to eat. A slight, humid breeze wafted through the screens. I hadn't heard Rusty come in last night. I knew he was at Shelly's.

At the table, Mom sliced her orange carefully and started neatly dividing the sections with the grapefruit knife. I sliced my grapefruit fast and sloppily, always in a hurry to eat and also hoping our "talk" wouldn't take too long. I wanted to get down to the shop.

"So," she began, "did you have a good time last night, walking the beach?" She emphasized the word, *beach*. Apparently she wanted me to notice the hint of sarcasm.

Heat burned up my neck into my cheeks. "Yeah, it was okay."

"And how is Sally?"

"She's fine." My mom liked Sally, most adults did. She looked innocent and had that blonde wide-eyed look down pat. But in reality, she sometimes smoked pot at parties and lied to her parents about a lot more than I ever did. Appearances could be deceiving, that was the point.

Skipper was chirping away from the open door of his white cage, trying to get our attention. "Skipper-dee...Skipper-dee," he murmured, over and over.

Mom sipped her coffee without saying anything for a moment. I could tell she was mulling over what to say next.

"Honey," she began, "look, I know I can trust you....it's just, well, this is a hard age. I remember what it's like, believe me. Making the wrong choices right now can mean real trouble for you-- a whole lifetime of problems later on. Do you understand what I'm saying?"

"Mnn-nn--" I said, feeling uncomfortable, and guilty.

"You know how much I love you. But, you know, I let too much slide with Rusty, with everything going on then. I just--well, thank God he seems to have come out of it okay.--but you, well, it sounds so stupid, but it's different for girls, Jamie. It really is. I just want you to feel you can talk to me, if you need to--will you?"

"Yes, Mom, really, I *will*." I couldn't help the note of impatience that crept into my voice.

"Okay. Okay...good." She looked hard at me, her smoky gray eyes narrowed, "Just, *be careful*...." She brushed her dark bangs, peppered (since Dad died) with thin glints of silver, off her face.

I nodded. "I will..."

"You know, at sixteen I wasn't perfect, either," she said, a smile beginning to curve up one corner of her mouth, "believe it or not..."

"You weren't?" I said, her smile catching at the corner of my lips too.

"Not quite..." she replied. Skipper chirped in, "BYE-BYE!" We both laughed, and the tension was lifted, at least for the moment. I was ready for my escape.

"Hey, mom," I ventured, "I'm going to the shop and then I planned on hitting the beach with Sally later, if that's all right...." I began picking my dishes up from the table and heading for the kitchen.

"Rusty's shop?" I could hear the suspicion in her voice. "Is that all you're eating?"

"Yeah," I replied.

"Since when did hanging around your brother's shop get so interesting?"

"I just thought I'd stop by and say hi, that's all."

"Weren't we just talking about something here?" she asked. I was glad I was in the kitchen, away from her probing eyes.

"Okay, okay Mom. The truth is...Rusty promised he would take me for a spin on the new 1100 he got in." I peeked my head into the room to look at her as I said it, to convince her I wasn't lying, but I was thinking, *that and Blue, of course.*

"--Oh, Jamie, you know how I feel about you riding on those things..."

"I promise, we'll be careful, we will. Rusty doesn't take chances with me on there, Mom, you know he doesn't."

"All right, all right, but wear a helmet and make it a short ride. And Jamie, I want you back here by five-thirty for dinner. You were out late last night, and I'd like you home tonight, here with your boring old mother. Deal?" She walked into the kitchen as I was rinsing my dishes and tossing the orange rind into the garbage disposal. She rested a hand on my shoulder.

"Yep, okay, Can I go now?" I asked.

"-- While you're at it, see what Rusty's plans are for dinner. I'm sure he isn't available, but just in case."

"Will do--" I figured Rusty would be going to the *Apple* again that night, but I didn't tell Mom that. I didn't want to hurt her feelings. Rusty was still living at home for Mom's sake, I guess, but he was never here anyway. Rusty's girlfriend Shelly had an apartment, and he was always over there. He worked long hours, too. It was just a matter of time before he moved out completely. I wished he would pay a little more attention to Mom, though. She would probably rather he lived at Shelly's, if he would visit her at home more often, have dinner with us once in a while.

I maneuvered my bike out of the carport, knowing I'd be all sweaty by the time I got to the shop, but I didn't have the guts to ask Mom for a ride. I needed to get out of the house by myself for awhile. It was a close call, talking about last night, and I felt guilty. But at the same time, I was relieved to be free.

Rusty's shop was about a mile and a half from our house. There was a small shopping center next door, with a gas station, a grocery store, and about five or six other stores. It was on a busy two-lane road that went out to the beach, a prime location. The guy that used to own the shop hired Rusty when he was fifteen. Frank Hannan was old and the shop wasn't doing well then; Rusty really turned it around. Very quickly, he got a reputation as the motorcycle whiz-kid. He could listen to a bike for a minute or two and know exactly what was wrong. He spent all his Saturdays and most of his evenings over there, except during football season. The old man really came to love Rusty, and he knew our dad had just died, so he took special interest in him. Everybody in town knew my Dad, and most of them loved him.

Lots of people in town had their houses or offices built by Dad's company, just because they liked him so much. He was funny and honest, was an amazing builder, and he had a real knack for getting along with all different kinds of people. He talked to the custodian at the school the same joking, friendly way he talked to the mayor. He was always helping people in town at no charge, if they needed a daycare playground built or the church painted. Practically the whole town had come to a standstill the day of his funeral. They were all there.

But my dad wanted Rusty to go to college, because he never did. Dad always read a lot. He was interested in astronomy and politics and history, and he was ashamed he wasn't "properly educated." But old man Hannan also loved Rusty, like the son he never had, and he left the shop to him when he died, years after Dad was gone.

I don't think Dad would have been satisfied with Rusty running *Hannan's Wheels*. He wanted more for him, for both of us. But that was what happened when people died. Lots of times, it changed the course of the people's lives who were left behind. Me, I knew I was not going to get stuck in Taraberg, Florida for the rest of my life. My grades were good, almost straight A's (except for math, which I hated). Mom always said I was different (although it wasn't clear if that meant good different or bad different). But I wasn't going to let anything stop me from going to college, preferably somewhere far away. I wrote and took pictures for the school paper and played second seed on the tennis team. I was also in every play the school had. But Taraberg wasn't where I wanted to stay. I dreamed of someplace glamorous, bigger, and far away. I dreamed of traveling and being famous—for what, I wasn't yet sure.

By the time I go to the shop, I was sticky and overheated. Luckily, Rusty had a coke machine where I could get an icy soda, one-and-a-half miles in ninety-five degree heat was a long way. I fanned my shirt in and out and pulled up to the coke machine right off.

I could see Tucker there already, near the office door, spread out in an old armchair. Tucker was big and rough looking: big legs, big chest, big arms, several tattoos, but most of the time he was like a teddy bear in nature. Sweet as could be. Tucker hated summer, though, with the extra weight he lugged around in the heat, he never stopped sweating. Rusty was in the garage bay with the door up. It was pretty cool in there, with all the cement and two big fans on the ceiling whirring away. The door to the office was propped open with a block of wood, so Tucker could give Rusty advice from the chair, not that he wanted it. Rusty had some tools spread out on the cement floor and three bikes lined up to work on. The new bikes out in front glinted in the sun, displayed where the tourists could see them on the way to the beach.

"Well, well, and why am I so honored?" Rusty said, looking up at me from where he lay on the floor.

"Hey Bro'...Tucker," I drawled.

"Little Sister, how's it goin'?" Tucker asked.

"Not too bad, Tuck, thanks. How's Joanie?"

Tucker just rolled his eyes.

"So, what is it you want, Baby?" Rusty knew I hated it when he called me that.

"I just wanted to come by and say, hey. See what was up," I replied, then took a huge gulp of my soda.

"I see you everyday, Jamie, at home, remember?"

"Hardly! You say good-bye as you're walking out the door. *If* you come home."

"--Oh no, you didn't come on a mission from Mom did you, to lecture me?"

"No...."

"--What then?"

"Well, Jeez, can't I even just come here for a real conversation with my brother for a change, without you thinking I'm *after* something?"

"Not likely, Jamie. You're always after something."

"Okay then, how about a ride on that sweet 1100 to the beach--or better yet, over to Sally's house? I want to show her," I said, figuring I would divert him.

"J -- I've got a million things to do today. And I wanted to hit the beach myself later this afternoon, if I ever get finished up here. Some of the guys are coming by. After that storm a few days ago, I guess the waves are still up." Rusty kept working away on the bike the whole time he was talking. It was second nature to him. Tucker was dozing off in the chair. The local rock station was blasting from the office radio, and I didn't know how he could sleep with all the noise. I guess he could sleep through anything. I wondered who the "guys" were, and if Blue was one of them.

"-- Oh, before I forget, Mom wants to know if you'll grace us with your presence at dinner tonight," I said, in my most snobby voice. "She says she's forgotten what you look like." I can be a real smart aleck when I want to be.

"-- Real funny, Baby. Can't, though, I gotta take Shelly out to eat. I promised...maybe tomorrow, tell her."

I shrugged. I knew he wouldn't. Just Mom and me for dinner again. "Well, can I at least get a ride out of this, Rusty? I mean, I rode all the way down here on my bike and everything."

"Oh man, Jamie, spare me the soap opera. Alright, alright, I'll take you for a spin. Will you just wait 'til I finish this, please? It's Blue's, and he's comin' by any minute to pick it up."

For one second, my heart felt like it squeezed shut completely. The room spun around and I think I gasped out loud. Luckily, Rusty was preoccupied and Tucker was dozing off in the chair, so no one noticed that I almost lost consciousness.

Blue's bike was a Honda 750, black with gold-chrome trim, lean and mean. I could just see Blue riding that bike... and me on the back. I could not believe this was just good luck, fate seemed to be calling. I knew I would meet Blue, I just knew it. I wondered what the story of his name was, anyway. Blue...a strange, beautiful name... I wanted to ask Rusty about it, but didn't dare. Rusty had an old car seat pushed up against the wall of the garage that was smeared with grease hand-prints and ripped up, but I needed to sit down. I sank to it and held the cold can of Pepsi against my forehead. Questions zipped through my brain: *When would he be there? What if he didn't come? What if he did? Who would he be with? Would he even notice me? What would I say?*

I couldn't let Rusty know. He was protective when it came to me, and I had a feeling Blue was not the kind of guy he wanted around his little sister.

"Damn it!" Rusty hissed. I jumped. He cut his finger on a loose wire and immediately sucked the blood out of it.

"God, Rusty, that's *so* gross," I said, trying to act normal. I examined Blue's bike as if it could reveal some secret, vital information about him. I wished it could talk.

It could have been anyone's bike, but it wasn't. It had a black leather seat - I loved the smell of leather--definitely big enough for two. I wondered how many girls had been on the back of that bike, but I didn't want to think about that. My imagination was running. Me on the back, arms around Blue's waist, my chest pressed against his back, my thighs snug up behind his, and the wind ripping through his blond curls. But, what would he see in me? I had to think of something... some way to get his attention. I was nowhere near as pretty as Patti. But I was a lot more interesting. If I could get him to talk to me a little, to see I had guts and heart and a brain, there might be a chance. I knew I could make him laugh anyway.

My mind reeled through all the old movies I'd seen. My mother had gotten me hooked on Bogart, Cary Grant and Hepburn and all the old classic movie stars. They always knew the perfect zinger line to say. Me, I tended to say exactly the wrong thing under pressure, to come out with some wisecrack that landed wrong.

"There," Rusty said, tossing the wrench back into his toolbox with a clank, "Finito."

As if on cue, a beat-up red Volkswagen van pulled into the lot. It seemed to be full of bodies, but I spotted a flash of Blue's unmistakable blond head from the garage. My face burned from the jolt of adrenaline that pulsed through my body, and I got instantly shaky. I hoped my legs would hold up as I stood and walked to the open door. I stopped, leaned against the door-jam of the garage bay, jutting my left hip out and slipping my hands into my front pockets, hoping to appear casual. I kept telling myself he probably wouldn't notice me anyway. I hated getting my hopes too high and then having them splattered on the rocks below. That had happened to me lots of times before. I told myself I would not ruin my whole day over it, no matter what happened.

Blue slid out of the passenger-side window. I guess the door was broken, but he pulled himself out of the car and landed in one fluid motion, like a cat. In the sunlight he seemed to radiate gold. I noticed that his hair was more gold than blond, and his skin tanned to a deep honey-brown, not the sun burnt red-brown a lot of people in Florida got. He had on a faded mint green tank top and jean cut-offs. His long tanned legs were flecked with gold hair. He had on dock-siders and no socks. I didn't know if I could handle seeing so much of his skin. I could barely breathe; he was so beautiful to look at.

The other guys in the van were hooting and shouting things at Rusty like, "Hey, man. How's it goin? Comin' surfin' later?" They left the van's motor running, and it was idling rough and loud. I could make out at least one female voice laughing shrilly from the back.

Tucker was roused from his heat-induced stupor by the commotion, and he waddled over to the van to talk with the crowd inside. He nodded a greeting at Blue. Blue and Rusty walked toward me, getting right into a conversation about his motorcycle. Blue stood only a few yards away from me now, and I wondered if he could feel the sparks lifting off my skin. Rusty's copper hair glinted in the sunlight and his freckles stood out like cinnamon sprinkles. The contrast of their heads side-by -side reminded me of Indian paintbrush flowers: one yellow, one orange. Blue still hadn't acknowledged my existence and my hope was beginning to slide.

I saw Blue gesture to his motorcycle and say something I couldn't hear. He and Rusty strolled over to it. Blue ran a hand over the seat as they talked, as if stroking the flank of a favorite horse. Suddenly his green eyes drifted up, looked over Rusty's shoulder, caught mine, and held. Everything else in the background blurred, there was only his eyes. So as not to interrupt the conversation, Blue didn't say anything to Rusty. He just kept those cool green eyes fastened onto mine. And something passed between us. I felt it, a jolt of connection, an invisible, electric current.

"Hey, Russ," he said after a long pause in conversation, still looking over Rusty's shoulder at me, "Who's this?" He nodded towards me, the green of his eyes the exact color of his shirt, piercing, eerie eyes. Tiger eyes. I couldn't look away. I smiled back, weakly.

Rusty glanced towards me, "Oh," he said dismissing me quickly, "That's just my little sister, Jamie. She came down here to beg a ride off me, as usual."

"Oh," Blue said, nodding, never taking those eyes off me, "Nice to meet ya....Little sister." His speaking voice was deeper than his singing voice, slightly rough. I loved the way he talked. I wanted to hear him talk some more. All day, if possible.

"You too," I said, swallowing hard. I had never felt dizzy just looking at someone.

"-- Yeah," Rusty said, " I promised I'd take her out before I get out of here and go catch some waves later. You going?"

Blue slowly pulled his eyes away from mine and looked back to Rusty. "Yeah, yeah, I probably will. Hey, listen," he said, "why don't I take her out, Russ? Kill two birds with one stone. I mean, I'd like to try my bike out anyway. I owe you a favor, man, we won't go far."

Rusty admired Blue so much; I prayed he wouldn't dare say no. Finally he shrugged and said, "Yah, right. Well, what the hell. But, take it easy, Blue. She's just a kid." Rusty looked at me when he said the last part, a look that said, *watch yourself.*

"Hey, have I ever let you down, Bud? " Blue said, swinging one beautiful long leg over his bike. Then he grinned and held his hand up to stop the reply, "'-Kay, don't answer that."

Rusty let out a snort of laughter, waved his hand in the air to dismiss us, and walked back into the shop. "Helmet, Jamie," he ordered. Blue nodded for me to get on the back.

He handed me the metallic blue helmet that was strapped to the rack behind his seat. It was unreal, like a mirage, but it was really happening. I was almost afraid to get on, afraid that touching him might make him evaporate, or make me dissolve into a glob of brainless jello. Not knowing quite what to do, I slipped on behind him and grabbed the leather handle straps along the edges of the seat, instead of onto Blue. I felt the heat of his warm thighs between mine. I pulled my feet up to the pedal sticks, which he kicked down smoothly for me. Blue revved the engine. Thanks to Rusty, it purred.

Blue eased out to the edge of the lot, and I decided I didn't care if we crashed and died the minute the ride was over. I would have been happy. I wanted to absorb every sight, sound, and gesture of those

15

minutes, so they would last the rest of my life if they had to. I wanted to smell Blue's skin up close and feel his body heat. If that was all I ever got, I decided it would be enough.

The red van honked its horn at us and pulled out into the traffic. Blue waved them on in front of us. They waved back, honked again and headed right onto the beach road. We went the other way. Blue handled the bike like a pro, with the same smooth ease that he handled his guitar. I didn't know anyone who had as much of a feel for motorcycles as Rusty did, but Blue came close. When we pulled up to the next red light, he reached back and pulled my arms around his waist. "It's better this way," he said, above the hum of the engine, "Safer. Hold on."

If it weren't for the bulbous helmet, I could have rested my cheek down on his shoulder blades. I pressed lightly up against him and peered at the world over Blue's shoulder, inhaling his scent, his blond curls ruffling close to my face. When the light changed, he kicked into gear and we zipped off fast.

Blue took another turn, and we ended up on the road to the beach again, but heading the opposite way the van had gone. The public beach was on a key, a small island attached to the mainland by two bridges. There were two keys off the coast of Taraberg, one was a bird and wildlife sanctuary and the other was Manatee Key, a tourist paradise, full of condominiums, fancy shops, bars, restaurants, and a beach that was listed as one of the world's top ten. The road we drove down wound along the coast of Manatee Key, past smaller beaches and inlets and eventually by the main beach, then back to the mainland across the other bridge.

Huge banyan trees arched over the road, draped with vines, Spanish moss and air-plants. We passed low clumps of palmettos and thick bushes of red hibiscus. Another row of flowering shrubs littered the road with pink and white blossoms. As we drove over the petals, they got caught in our wind, swirling up around us like pink snow. The sun slanted down through the holes in the trees overhead. The heat was broken by the shade and our own wind. I was so high from the sunlight and the speed and just being close to Blue, I thought I might die of happiness. For that moment, life was as perfect as it ever got.

The houses that lined this section of the Key were old and they sat back in thick jungle growth, partially hidden from the road. Most had gates barring long crushed white shell driveways, keeping out the outside world. They all had beachfront views of the Gulf. Someday, I wanted to buy one of those houses for my mother.

As we flew along, I kept reminding myself it was Blue driving. It was really him, the guy I had dreamed about only last night. He smelled warm, clean like soap, coconut suntan oil and something else delicious, just *him*.

16

In a way it was good that we couldn't talk, because of the helmet, the engine whine and the speed. We just cruised on, pressed close, skin warm, our bodies talking. I was painfully, blissfully aware of every place we touched.

Once you've ridden on a motorcycle with someone, you can't help but feel you know them better. You can't share that particular ride with anyone else. It's just between the two of you, what you saw and where you went. We leaned into the corners and sped up on the straight-aways. It was the closest thing to flying that I know. I never wanted to stop.

But we had passed the beach and were heading back across the other bridge, completing the loop. Rusty's shop was only a mile away. I couldn't help but wonder what would happen next, and when or if Blue would ever be alone with me again. At least he asked me to go this once—and that was something. And the way he had looked at me and the heat passing between our bodies--that was something too.

I could see the entrance to Hannan's. "Better get you back, Darlin'!" he called over his shoulder. I couldn't believe he had said it, *darlin'*. I wanted to hear him call me that again, and again, and again.

We pulled into the driveway, and he coasted right up to the garage. Rusty was inside working on another bike. He glanced up at us and then back down again. I slid off the back and Blue grabbed my hand, squeezed it, and forced me to catch his eyes. He smiled at me, his slow dazzling smile, like sunlight bouncing off the surface of a lake. I smiled back, mumbled "thanks," and handed him the helmet. He strapped it on in a smooth practiced motion, winked at me and pulled away. I stood frozen.

"Well," said Rusty. "Have a good ride?" He kept working on the bike, apparently unaware of my dazed condition.

"Yeah..." I answered. "*Great* ride. So... that's Blue."

"Yep, and the punk took off without paying me. Oh well, I'll catch him later. It was no big deal to fix anyway."

"Where's Tucker?" I asked.

"I dunno...he took off."

"Well, I guess I'll take off, too," I said.

"Now that you got your ride, right?" Rusty said, looking up at me from under his eyebrows, the way he did sometimes when he was about to give me advice. I made a face at him and started to go over to my bike.

"Hey," Rusty said quietly, pausing as he wiped a rag across his wrench.

I looked at him. "Yeah?"

"Listen, I'm not telling you what to do, J." He looked down, still rubbing the wrench. "But Blue is...Well, just don't go floating off over him.

Don't get me wrong--I like him. He's a friend, man. But, he likes girls, Jamie, and a lot of other things, too. He's a lot older than you. So just don't go thinking it means anything to him, that's all. Do you get what I'm saying to you?" He pointed the wrench at me, his gray-blue eyes blazing and I knew he meant it.

I nodded and said, "Yeah, I get it." I wondered what was it about being sixteen that invited so much unwanted advice, first Mom, and then Rusty. Besides, it was too late. I couldn't tell Rusty that I was already floating. I was long gone. I waved good-bye and started home.

I re-lived the motorcycle ride over and over as I pedaled, so the mile home was a blur. I didn't even notice time passing until I pulled onto our street. But by the time I got there, I knew what I had to do. How could I explain to my brother about the pull of the current that passed between Blue and me? I felt it, and saw it in his eyes. I had to see where it would take me, I just had to. Even if it meant paying a price as I drifted downstream.

CHAPTER THREE

At the beach, the afternoon after my ride with Blue, I recounted every detail of my two meetings with Blue to Sally, at least three times. We walked up and down the beach to check out who was surfing. But the rest of that day was dull by comparison.

Sally liked older guys, especially surfers, so we tried to look casual as we waded by them, shin-deep in the water, sucking in our stomachs. We saw Rusty and some of his other friends and we waved, but I didn't see Blue anywhere. I wondered how long it would be before I saw him again. Sally said she hoped it would be soon because she wasn't sure she could stand me. It was a typical Florida day, gorgeous, hot, the sun bouncing off the white sugar-sand and the topaz water so hard it made your eyes hurt. Sunglasses were a necessity. We picked up a few unusual shells as we walked, even though we already had a hundred at home. For us, it was just another day at the beach.

We lay on our beach towels, talking lazily and checking our tan lines. We played around in the Gulf for at least an hour. We talked with a few friends who strolled by, but decided not to play in the everyday summer-long volleyball game, as we sometimes did. I was still kind of dreamy from the morning ride, I guess, because I kept thinking I saw Blue everywhere, but it was never him. After awhile we packed up for home. Sally had her dad's car, the Volvo, which for some reason, we nicknamed the Go-go.

While Sally drove, recklessly as usual, she tried to convince me to come with her and two other sophomore guys to a drive-in movie that night. One of the guys, David, had a van Sally really liked, with thick lime green carpet inside and a great stereo. I teased her about liking the van better than she liked David, because he only seemed to be her date when she couldn't get anyone "better," as she put it. After being with Blue, I had no desire to go out with a boring sophomore named Mark. He was nice and all that, I told Sally, but no thanks. Besides, I had promised Mom I'd stay home that night.

Sally rolled her eyes and said she could see I was going to be a whole lot of fun that summer. She dropped me off and peeled off, mad. But I wasn't worried. I knew she would probably find someone else to go with, and if not she would still be over it by tomorrow. Sally and I had been best friends since fourth grade.

Mom and I had a quiet dinner. I cooked the hamburgers and roasted the corn in their husks on the grill, while Mom tossed a salad and set the table in the lanai. We talked about our days. I told her everything, except the part about Blue.

When I told her in the kitchen that Rusty wouldn't be home, she got the familiar hurt look in her eyes and turned away for minute. Then she shrugged her shoulders and said, "Well, let's eat then."

I just couldn't tell her about Blue, not yet. It was still too new, too uncertain, and also, somehow sacred. I only had that one magical ride with him and although it wasn't much, it was mine. I wanted to savor it. I knew she would worry. She had heard all about Blue from Rusty and his crowd. The guys used to spend a lot of time hanging out at our house, before Rusty graduated and got so serious with Shelly. Mom didn't really know Blue, but she had heard about him. I knew she would say he was too old for me and too wild. So I left the motorcycle ride out.

We talked about Rusty for a while. She asked if I got my ride and I started to blush. I recovered, said I did, and that it was fine. Now I would have to make sure Rusty didn't blow my cover, somehow.

I hated the way it was getting so difficult to have a simple conversation with my mother without lying. I didn't like it, but I didn't know exactly what to do about it either. I couldn't stop seeing Blue, and I couldn't tell my mother I was seeing him. Those were the two indisputable facts. So the tension hung over us and guilt followed me from room to room, like a stray dog, whenever my mother and I were in the house together. It hung over our dinner that night, too. Even though everything was the same, Mom and I eating together and talking, something had altered slightly, like a subtle shift in the wind.

Afterwards we played a few hands of gin rummy, like we usually do, and watched an old Jimmy Stewart movie, my favorite one, *The Philadelphia Story*. But part of me just wasn't there. I kept drifting to the *Apple* in my mind, watching Blue up on stage teaching those strings to talk. I couldn't help but wonder who was at the *Apple* that night, if Patti was there, and what I might be missing. That was the problem with falling for someone -- it made you care too much.

CHAPTER FOUR

The next morning, I had some work to do. I mowed ten or twelve lawns a week in the summer and made pretty good money doing it. It came out to about two or three lawns a day. We lived in a large development and since I had to push the mower from lawn to lawn, it was a good thing the houses were close together. I charged ten dollars a cut, so I ended up with about four-hundred bucks or more at the end of the month. Not bad.

There were tons of landscapers in Florida, so competition was tough. That was why I kept my prices low. It was big business and year round. People were much more meticulous about their lawns than they were up North. It was hard, hot work. But I liked the smell of fresh-cut grass, working my body, and letting my mind wander as the mower hummed away. All that walking and pushing kept me in good shape. Of course the drawback was that it was never really done. You had to keep coming back, week after week, all summer, swatting bugs and fighting against the grinding heat, doing the same lawns until you felt like you could cut them in your sleep. So there wasn't much challenge or job satisfaction. But all in all, it was a pretty good summer job. I told Mom that when I saved up enough money, maybe I'd buy a riding mower. I could do a lot more lawns that way and exert less effort. But secretly, I kind of liked the rhythm of walking.

Naturally, as I walked back and forth, back and forth, sweating under my favorite old straw panama hat, I found myself thinking about Blue. I wondered what he did in the summer to make money. I was sure he didn't make enough playing guitar. I wondered what his parents were like and what he did all day. I figured he must have another job. Rusty had implied his family situation wasn't great, but I didn't know what that meant. He had graduated with Rusty two years before, and it surprised me that Blue hadn't left town. I wondered what he liked to eat and do: I wanted to know everything. I pushed the mower across the Stevens' lawn automatically.

I knew my customers' lawns like my own. I had been cutting most of them since I was twelve. Sometimes, someone came out and offered me a glass of iced tea or something cold to drink, which was great.

But I liked it even better when one of them went away on vacation and told me I could swim in the pool if I wanted, while they were gone. We didn't have a pool. A lot of people in our neighborhood did. Nothing felt better than a plunge into a cool, screened-in pool after cutting lawns all morning in ninety-nine degree heat, nothing.

One time after I cut the Williams' lawn, I went skinny-dipping, without permission, in their pool. They lived on a huge corner lot, so no one could see into their backyard. The large stucco Spanish-style house sat back from the road and the yard was rangy and wild on the edges, with lots of big palm and live oak trees draped with Spanish moss. I saw a pygmy rattler in that yard once, and I still watch my step around there.

But that day I really thought I might pass-out in the heat. When I finally finished mowing their giant lawn, I staggered to the lanai and took the key from where they'd showed me it was kept, under the geranium pot. I let myself in and stripped out of my clothes so fast, I don't think anyone could have made much out even if they had seen me. My clothes were soaked through. I knew the Williams wouldn't be home until the next day, they were away, and that pool had been calling to me the whole time I was cutting. I never felt a swim as close to heaven as that one. My whole body, every pore of skin, drank the cool water in and came back to life. I floated, with my face to the sky for a long time. Sometimes we have to take heaven where we can find it, at least that's my motto.

I smiled, remembering, while I dripped sweat and finished up the Stevens' lawn. It was crazy all the people in Florida who had pools and never used them. If I had one, I would have been in it all day. Though I had to admit, there was something even more tantalizing about the real turquoise water and soft white sand of the Gulf, and that was all mine for the taking.

When all the lawns for that day were done, I pushed my clackety old mower down the street towards home. I had just enough energy left to make it back; I needed water, food and a swim to revive me. My legs, back and arms were aching.

I wondered what Sally was up to. Her parents were rich, so they told her she didn't have to work until she was eighteen, lucky dog. Her father was a doctor and her mother was an art professor. Sally had one older sister in college up North. Sally got spoiled a lot, being the youngest. I decided not to call her. I felt like going to the beach by myself for a change. Just some quiet time to think and relax in the sun was what I needed, not a lot of chit-chat. But I dreaded the thought of the three-mile bike ride to the beach.

I shoved the mower into the carport and went inside. I couldn't wait to get my driver's license in the fall, that would be true freedom. I hoped mom was home, maybe I could convince her that I would die if she didn't drive me to the beach. I wondered if she would even be in the mood for a swim with me -- we hadn't done that in awhile. That would make me feel less guilty about lying lately, anyway. I hollered hello as I went in and made straight for the kitchen to pour myself a huge glass of ice tea. She called back to me from the yard, where she was hanging some clothes up on the line. I took two glasses of tea out to talk.

"Hi dear, you look melted," she said, as I handed her the drink.

I groaned, set my drink down, and flopped onto the white chaise lounge.

"How about a swim?" she asked.

"Oh, God, you read my mind. My mother is a genius."

"Well, I wouldn't go quite that far," she said. "And remember what I said about saying God?"

"--You said he's always watching me."

"--Jamie, you know what I mean."

"I know, sorry."

"I'm almost done here, why don't you go change," she said, hanging a pair of my shorts on the line.

"Help me," I said, reaching my arm out to her as feebly as I could, "I'm drowning in my own sweat."

"That's gross, Jamie, now move it," she slapped me lightly on the palm. She picked up the laundry basket and took it inside, and I got up to follow her.

After a quick sandwich and a change, I was out in the car before Mom was. Just to be a pain, I beeped the horn. She came out of the house with her beach- bag and a towel draped over her shoulder. She gave me a look that said, if you weren't my daughter I'd kill you.

We chatted on the way, and I was glad I decided to go with her after all. I didn't spend as much time with her as I used to, and I'd forgotten that my mom could be kind of fun. She had me laughing with her stories about the people in the dentist's office. We had our differences, but all in all, I had to admit I was glad she was my mom. We talked about the patients she liked and the ones she hated to see come in. We talked about my lawn business. She was proud of me for the job I'd done with it and for keeping it up all these years. When I started, I only had five lawns a week.

After we parked and trudged across the scorching sand in our flip-flops, we found a spot close to the water to plop our stuff down.

23

The Gulf looked too good to be true. I remembered in New Hampshire the water was dark grey-green some days, blue-black on others, and so cold your feet went numb when you waded in it. It was amazing to live in place where the beach looked just like the ones you saw in magazines: scattered palm trees, clear turquoise water and blinding white silky sand. Granted, we had red tide outbreaks once in awhile that coated the beach in red slime, and occasional schools of stinging jelly-fish that drifted in -- but still, the Gulf water was to me, always the sweetest of invitations. I couldn't wait to get in.

Mom and I dropped our towels in the sand and, without talking, ambled straight for the water. Before I knew it, we were laughing and racing each other. My mom can still run pretty fast -- she even jogs once in awhile. But of course, I beat her. She wasn't that fast. I dove under with my arms stretched in front of me. Sweet relief. I pulled down through the clear aqua water and gripped two fistfuls of the cool sand on the bottom, and let it sift through my fingers as I pushed up for air.

Mom surfaced just a few feet away and began her steady, strong crawl out to sea.

"Write when you get to Cuba!" I yelled after her. But she didn't hear me. I knew she'd swim out and parallel to the beach, get a good work out and come back in. She loved swimming even more than I did. I didn't feel like exerting myself that much after traipsing back and forth over all those lawns, so I basked in the warm buoyant blue, floating on my back for a while, with my face to the sun.

Finally ready to get out, I waded slowly towards the beach, the water tugging at my thighs. The dip had revived me. But what I saw just a hundred feet down the water's edge, struck me like a blow to the head. It was Blue... walking away from me with Patti Jansen. You couldn't mistake his hair or her wiggle from the back. She wore a white bikini made of very little material. It contrasted starkly with her tanned skin and shiny black hair. Blue was holding her hand in his.

He wore lemon colored trunks and nothing else. His skin was gold, hers mahogany. They were like something out of a travel to tropical paradise ad. Patti was looking over at him and smiling adoringly from time to time, while she listened to him talk. I thought I might throw up and blood rushed to my face. I wanted to sink down, down under the sand, until I was covered by hot gritty granules, safe and silent as a crab underneath.

For all appearances, Blue and Patti were made for each other. I tried to rationalize the pain that ripped through my stomach. The hot, sick ache that flooded through me. He had a right to mess around with girls.

24

After all, he hardly knew me, and I was four years younger than he was. It wasn't like he had promised me anything. But the nausea still swelled up, thick and syrupy, into the back of my throat.

I spread my towel out on the sand as quick as I could and flopped face down. I cradled my head on my arms, shielding my face in the crook of an elbow, pretending I was asleep, and praying he wouldn't see me. My scalp prickled with humiliation. Swimming had been so good, I was happy. Having it ripped away from me so suddenly felt like cheating. My mom kept telling me she didn't know where I got the idea that life was fair. She said she never promised me that. But I still kept looking, blindly, for things to work out. Except lots of times, they just didn't, like with dad. Then I'd be disappointed and stunned, over and over again. I was dumb like that I guess.

Although I was sick with the notion, I felt compelled to look down the beach to see if Blue and Patti were stretched out nuzzling each other on a towel. The same morbid impulse that made you have to see - yet avoid seeing- a bad car wreck. But I was so afraid it might be really happening, that I forced myself to keep my eyes closed and tried to concentrate on the sun beating down on the back of my legs and shoulders.

I was so blind-sided that I was unaware of how much time passed before my mom came back from her swim. Beads of water that still clung to her skin and green suit dripped down onto her towel as she spread it out and lay beside me. "Ah," she said, "just what I needed."

I was still trying to blot out the picture of Patti and Blue behind my eyes. I definitely didn't want Patti in my head, and I wasn't sure if I wanted Blue there anymore either.

"How was your swim, Hon'?" Mom asked, settling on her back, face to the sun.

"Fine... great."

Mom, with her usual radar detection, picked her head up and squinted over at me. "So, what's up?"

"Nothing. Really. I'm fine."

"Sure?"

"Yeah...the water was great. I guess I'm just not in a talking mood...Maybe I'll just close my eyes for a minute, take a nap." I was trying to put mom's mind at ease, but I wasn't sure I could muster the effort it took to do it.

We both fell quiet for a long time. Mom fell asleep, I think, and the sun felt good seeping into me. But I couldn't get rid of it, the image of them walking along the water's edge together, holding hands. I hoped they would be far, far away by the time I had to get up and leave the beach. I should have expected it. How naive of me. After what Rusty said, the way Patti was looking at Blue the other night at the *Apple*, it should have come as no surprise. So why did it hit me like a blow to the stomach?

Because... I felt special with Blue, and about him, that was why. I thought he was different. I didn't want him to turn out to be like all the other guys I knew. Most of them were just boys. They chased girls who put out, and tried to act tough and cool all the time. When they got into a pack they would get loud and shovey, trying to impress each other, and the girls, by bragging. There seemed to be nothing they wouldn't do or say to show off. They'd sock at each other and make snide remarks about sex.

When I knew, for a fact, half of them hadn't even done it. A couple of them, with their steady girlfriends, but around their guy friends they sometimes even said rude things about their own girlfriends. Yea, I had been around guys a lot. I knew how they thought, how they acted. I had a lot of those guys as friends, but I wasn't interested in going out with any of them I knew, even though I dated a few of them once or twice. But I had been waiting for someone different. I didn't want Blue to be like them. When he played that guitar, he had something special, a true gift. He had to have magic inside him to write and play like that, and deeper thoughts and feelings than the guys I knew. He just had to.

So I didn't want him to waste his time on girls like Patti. Sure, I was young and maybe not as pretty, but I bet I had things to say to him that would make him think, and maybe even make him laugh. I wanted a guy who would look at me with a shine in his eyes. Not just for the way I looked, but for who I was. All Patti talked about was her hair, the next party, her clothes, shallow, stupid things like that. About nothing. I wanted Blue to be the kind of guy who wanted more than that. Maybe I had been wrong about him. Maybe he was just like all the rest. But even while my head was trying to blow him out my mind forever, like a speck of worthless dust, my heart was holding him in.

CHAPTER FIVE

I didn't see Blue again until three weeks later. I had been to the beach thinking I might run into him, but pride was holding me back from really seeking him out. I was stubborn, and I wasn't too keen on the idea of seeing him with Patti again anyway. Without even realizing it, he had let me down, and part of me never wanted to see him again. But another part -- the stupid part -- wondered if Patti truly had her hooks in him yet. And his music wouldn't leave me alone.

I found myself humming tendrils of songs while I mowed lawns, or put away laundry, or stepped into the shower. I woke up in the morning with a string of notes twisting through my mind, and they were Blue's notes. More than anything (even talking to him), I wanted to hear him sing and play again. I craved it, like the craving I got for chocolate sometimes. I couldn't stop wanting it. Besides, something told me I had not yet played out my hand. Something told me, it was far from over between us.

I finally decided to go halfway. To satisfy my hunger for his music, I would walk down to the *Apple* Friday night, but I vowed I would stand outside and listen if I had to. I would not go in and let him see me there for the price of the moon. And I would take Sally with me, for camouflage. She told me I was crazy if I thought I could go there by myself, anyway. After all my talk, she wanted to hear and see him too, although I hadn't even mentioned his name since that sickening day at the beach.

It was a hot, orangey twilight wrapped in blue tissue paper. Strands of the sunset still hung in the night sky like whispers of smoke, the way Blue's music hung in my mind. As I swung by Sally's house, I hummed one of his tunes. We each told our parents we were going to a movie, which we were, after we stopped off to listen for a while.

I rapped on the wood of Sally's screen porch door. I heard her holler, "Bye!" and come down the stairs. Sally was pretty, and she knew it. She had on tight white jeans and a black-and-white striped shirt that bared her midriff. The puffy short sleeves kept sliding off her shoulder periodically. She would casually pull each one back up, as if it all happened by accident. Seeing her step onto the porch, I began to wonder if it was a good idea to let Blue see Sally after all. Her soft blonde hair rippled down her back, and she flipped it every so often, for effect. In the summer, her hair bleached almost white in the sun.

We set off for the *Apple* with Sally doing most of the talking. I was content to listen, as I was preoccupied with thoughts of Blue. She went on and on about her parents and how dumb they were, how they embarrassed her, and smothered her, and how she couldn't wait to get out of the house in three years.

I didn't complain about my mother the way many of my friends did. With only one parent, I realized that I better appreciate what I had. Not that she didn't drive me crazy sometimes. But we drove them nuts, too, a lot of the time. I figured we were stuck with them for the duration, and then when we were free, we would miss them. To me, it seemed like a waste of time to moan about how bad it was. Sally's older sister was away at college and the first three or four months there, she was so homesick she called practically every day, and she "couldn't wait to get away" from her parents either. So I just listened when Sally went on like that and nodded as if I was agreeing with her.

It was a beautiful, sultry night with a humid Gulf breeze. I was just breathing the air and admiring the fading colors of the sky and waiting to lay my eyes on Blue again. It was the kind of night that made you want to do something crazy or wild, like skinny-dipping in the ocean or whooping out in the hot darkness from the open window of a car. Or better yet, taking a fast motorcycle ride along the Gulf.

When we got close to the *Apple*, my stomach grew tight and jangly. It was quiet in the street outside the *Apple*, though we could hear the thudding of the bass notes and drums vibrating through the walls. Most of the people who were going in were already inside. We had to keep an eye out so that none of Rusty's friends saw us. Not that they could do anything, we'd only be standing outside. But I knew Rusty would have a fit if I was anywhere near the place, and he would know exactly why I was there.

Except Sally was not the type to be shoved into the background. She was used to first-class treatment and people noticing her. What she didn't understand was that sometimes it was an advantage in life to know how to blend.

"Jaa--mie," she whined, when I led her to the side door off the main street, "What we going way back here for?"

"Look, Sal, if you want to see Blue, you have to come back here. If my brother sees you or me here, there will be no future for us, do you understand? He'd end it. You do want to live, don't you?"

"Oh, Rusty, he's just a big red-haired baby. I'm not afraid of him."

"Yeah, you think so? Well, you've never seen him mad, kiddo."

"--But..."

"--Sal, you wanna see Blue or not?" I said, growing exasperated.

"Yeah..."

"Well then, it's this way or no way. Besides, we can hear better from this door. It's closer to the stage."

I led her quickly to the fire-escape and we hiked up the flight of stairs to the stage door, our footsteps twanging with each step. I saw Blue's Honda chained to the bottom of the railing.

"Look Madame," I said, sweeping my hand out, making a big show of her seat on top of the fire-escape landing. "We even have our own private balcony seats." We did have a clear side-view down a long, dark hall to the stage, just as I had hoped. The door was wide open. It was a perfect secret vantage point.

"Oh God," Sally grumbled. "This is tacky, sitting out here like some stray dog above the garbage dumpster...and from this far away, I'll barely see him at all, and from just *one* side!" She looked down at the stair disgustedly and wiped the flank of her white jeans before sitting. I hoped the rust wouldn't stain them or she'd have a tantrum for sure.

While Sally was whining, I picked out Blue's voice from the mumbles and laughter of noise that flowed out toward us. The canned music had been stopped and he was about to begin. "Shush-Shush," I said, "that's him." Sally stopped whining for a change.

"Evening folks..." His voice melted down through the layers of my skin, right to my bones. "My name's Blue," he went on. There was a lot of whistling and clapping in response and shouts of "Yeah, we know!" from his friends. I could imagine him grinning, that cool sexy smile out at them, even though I was too far away to see his face clearly. But I could see his lean frame, his guitar strapped on, standing on the stage under the fall of the yellow spotlight.

"I'd like to play a tune I wrote that seems to fit a night like this..." he added, shifting his feet and rearranging the acoustic guitar strap over his shoulder. "It's called 'Sundown Mood.'" The first chord vibrated in my stomach, washing over my nerves like a warm wave. It was jazzy and bluesy at once, with a slow, tantalizing rhythm.

Night wind, don't bring me no relief
too late for walking
too hot for sleep...

Why 'd you leave me with
these empty sheets
and a room full of blues...

Sally was barely breathing next to me. She didn't say one word as she listened, but I could see the effect he was having. Her chin was cradled in her hands, elbows propped on knees, and her ice-blue eyes fixed somewhere off in the night. She had forgotten all about the rusty steps. Me, I was watching his every move through the open door, getting lost again in the pulse and strum of his guitar and the soulful sound of his voice.

It may not have been the same as being inside, but what flowed out to us touched me like silk. The stars began to glitter against the blue-black sky, as if Blue had orchestrated it to provide a backdrop for the song. His music filled me with such a sweet ache. The rise and fall of his voice and the rhythm of his guitar hit me hard and deep. They were songs filled with loss and longing, and I knew it was coming from somewhere inside him. I wanted to touch that pool of hurt inside, to spread it out and away from him, to massage him free of it. Yet I also knew it was probably what made his music beautiful, and I couldn't help but wonder where it came from.

He launched into the solo and although I was too far away to see clearly, I could imagine his fingers walking those strings, as if I were standing right beside him. I could feel the sweat beading in his blond sideburns and on his forehead, see his lips pressed into a thin line of concentration. I could imagine his biceps flexing under the short sleeves of his shirt, and his downcast eerie-green eyes watching the strings and then looking out, but not really even seeing the faces of the crowd. He went someplace far away when he played. Even though I was way down the hall, I almost felt for that moment, I was him, inside his skin. Like I could share his thoughts, feel my own fingers entwined in his, bending those notes, stroking the strings. It was strange how tightly I felt connected to him. But then the song ended and the feeling evaporated like the tendrils of smoke in a fan.

First, there was silence. Then slowly, we heard the build of shrill whistles and raucous applause, until the whole building was vibrating with the sound of it. We felt it buzzing up through the metal stairs.

"Wow..." was all Sally said.

"Told you," I said.

"Yeah, I see what you mean...he's *real good.*"

30

"Wait until you *see* him," I said, hoping Sally wouldn't like what she saw too much. That worried me a little, I had to admit.

"Well, can't you *do* something? I mean, I want to see him--not from a million miles away, but up close. He looks cute from here, but can't we meet him somehow?"

"Not now, Sally. We better get to the movies...he's around. You'll see him at the beach one day."

"But I don't want to leave yet," Sally whined. "Can't we sneak in? I'd love a rum and coke right about now."

Sally was the last person I would sneak in anywhere with. She was too conspicuous. Besides, I was nervous being so close to the stage door with Blue's Honda right below us. It meant he had come up that way, and might be back again soon. I didn't want to get caught like that. And I had to admit, I was afraid he might pay more attention to Sally than to me, and that would be more than I could take. If I was going to see him, I wanted it to be just the two of us, on my own terms. I had enough competition with Patti panting after him; I didn't need my best friend catching his eye too. It wasn't fair that I wasn't as pretty as they were. But there wasn't much I could do about that. I just had to hope that Blue would see something different in me. But I didn't want him to accidentally glance down the hall and catch us skulking around on the fire escape like little kids, that much I knew.

Of course, Sally ignored me and stepped cautiously inside the doorway to the dimly lit hallway. She crossed her arms and leaned against the dingy, wood-planked wall, settling in.

"Sally," I hissed at her. "Get back out here!"

But when we heard Blue's voice again, my impulse to get out of there weakened. "I'm gonna change the mood a bit here," Blue went on, "and I'd like to invite a couple guys up to the stage, some old friends I used to play with in Tampa once in awhile. Some of you may know them...y'all know Sunstreak?" There were some scattered whistles and applause in recognition of the name. I knew then I had to stay to hear them. "So c'mon up, guys."

The drummer had a brown afro and a chunky body, and was the first to amble up onto the stage to the drum set, which had been assembled earlier, behind Blue. Then two other guys climbed up and went to their instruments. The tall one, all bone and angles, picked up the bass. He had shoulder-length black hair and a scraggly mustache. The other guy, who was retrieving his sax from its case, was black and huge, his biceps as big around as Blue's thighs. He wasn't fat, not an ounce of fat on him. But he was massive. He was all in white, his clingy pants hugging the bulging muscles in his thighs. He stood to Blue's right on the stage, almost blocking our view of him. It was a small stage, and they were all pretty crowded up there. His sax gleamed as he held it, shooting off silver sparks when it moved in the light. The bass player was still fiddling with his guitar, adjusting his foot pedal and the wires to his amplifier. When everyone finally had their equipment ready, they nodded their okay to Blue. Without any introduction, on Blue's count, they launched into a hard-driving version of "Midnight Hour."

It was clear they had played together before the way it all spilled together like colors in a paint box mixing, to create a new color all together.

It was tight and syncopated, and Sally and I couldn't stand still. I had never heard Blue sing with a band behind him. His rock voice was sexy and bluesy, almost growling, in contrast to the smooth-sweet way he sang his ballads. And the sax jumped in at just the right places, adding clean, crying notes of spice. I felt it deep in my belly. We were standing, swaying, and slapping our thighs to the beat. By this time, I had inched into the hallway too. It was cooler there than outside, and smelled of old wood, a dank but familiar smell. Sally had her eyes on the sax player, I could tell. I sighed a little, relieved that she had another interest besides Blue. But that guy could have crushed her with one squeeze, and he was also at least nineteen. I could just imagine her parents' reaction if she brought *him* home. But then again, Blue was three years older than me, so who was I to say.

When the song ended, the crowd went crazy, stomping and chanting.

Blue tried to quiet them, holding up his hand, but it still took them a while to calm down. "Hey, thanks!" he yelled. "Since y'all liked that so much, I'm gonna let these guys rock you for a song on their own...but I'll be right back!"

Before Sally or I could move, he waved, set his guitar down on its stand and ran down the hall toward us--as Sunstreak kicked into another song without him, the bass player singing lead. I don't know who was more startled when he almost crashed into us, him or us.

He stretched his arms out, putting a hand on each side wall, to block us off or steady himself, I wasn't quite sure. He was breathing hard and the sharp, salty smell of him filled the hallway, making me dizzy with desire. The rollicking back-beat of Sunstreak thumped behind him. "Well, well, and what do we have here?" He shouted, to be heard over the song.

"Ahh....Hey, Blue..." I shouted back. Sally stood looking up at him like some blonde-ice princess, stuck to the floor.

"Hey, yourself. What are y'all doin' back here?" He was grinning at us slyly, like he was in on the joke. "Hidin' out from big bad brothers, by any chance?"

I just nodded in response and a stupid terrified grin practically split my face.

"Well, whatta you know? Little sister's a wild one, I see--don't worry darlin', I like that in a woman." He was leaning over me now, grinning, his tiger eyes fixed on mine, and all I could think of was him pressing me up against the wall, grabbing my face in his beautiful long-fingered hands and kissing me, hard. He didn't, but he sure had edginess to him, a way of keeping me off-balance. I never could tell what he was going to do next. It was terrifying and thrilling at the same time.

"Sorry, Blue. I really am," I managed to eek out of dry lips. "It's just that, well, the door was open and--"

"--Hold on, girl--I'd be the last one to tell on you...." he grinned at me, obviously getting a kick out of the whole thing. "So... who's your blonde friend?" he asked loudly, nodding toward Sally.

"Oh--Sally, this is Blue." I introduced them.

"Pleased to meet you," Blue said, smiling his killer smile down on Sally. "C'mon," he said, tossing his head to indicate that we should move outside, where we wouldn't have to yell.

As soon as we were out on the fire-escape, he reached into his denim shirt pocket and pulled out a cigarette. He offered one to both of us and I couldn't believe it when Sally took one. I threw her a nasty look, saying, *you don't even smoke*. She made a face back, shrugging, as if to say, *I'll do what I want*. She looked up at Blue as he lit it for her, her famous wide-eyed *protect me* look that no boy I knew could resist. I hated her for it. Here stood the first guy I ever really wanted in my life, and my best friend was trying to steal him. But Blue didn't seem to notice. He turned to look back at me, exhaling a thick plume of smoke.

The sky was clear and dark now; it was a fragrant balmy night. I worried that we would soon miss the start of the movie. But somehow I didn't want to be anywhere else in the world, except there on the rusty fire-escape with Blue's eyes on mine.

"Whew, feels better out here," he said, smiling at me, leaning back on the railing and raking his hand back through his wavy hair in a gesture I already knew, from watching every move he made. "So, you girls snuck up here," he said, his voice teasing. "And what made you want to do that?"

"I--uh, we..." I started. "We wanted to hear you," I said quickly, preventing Sally from opening her big mouth.

"Me?" he said, pointing toward his chest with his cigarette. "You snuck up here to see me?"

I nodded.

"No kidding..." he murmured, "...and who told you I was worth seeing?"

"My brother, and well, just around," I replied. "We heard you were good."

"You did...and so, what *do* you think, little--it's Jamie, right?" He squinted at me, leaning against the railing taking another drag. He looked at me like what I said really mattered.

"Right, Jamie," I replied, "I think you're--"

Sally tossed her hair back over her shoulder and cut in breathlessly, "—Great, we think you are so *unbelievably* great..."

Blue laughed and looked at Sally and I wanted to kill her. "Well, thank you M'am," he said. We could still hear the gorgeous wail of the saxophone and the pulse of Sunstreak inside. "So, you ladies stayin' then? Cause I gotta run back inside to play some more, before I get my set break. Just wanted to cop a smoke. But if you're gonna hang out, well, maybe I can see you later."

"Can't," I replied, shaking my head. Wanting desperately to stay, but not wanting to explain about the movie, my mother and brother, curfews, and all that complicated a sixteen year old's life.

Then he said, still looking at me, but almost talking to himself, "Quite a little something, you are," his eyes dancing, almost mocking. "Never knew Rusty had a sister...and such a cute one," he grinned, making a hot flush rise to my cheeks.

Flustered, I blurted, "Yeah, well, he was probably trying to keep you away from me," and then instantly regretted it. I was always doing that, blurting out idiotic things when I was nervous.

Blue let out a burst of laughter. "And I can see why," he said, still grinning. "So, where are you ladies rushing off to?"

"Ah, we've got to meet some people...at the movies," I replied, lying. Blue's eyes and mine were catching each other and holding, and it was making it hard for me to concentrate.

"Oh, big date, huh?" he cocked an eyebrow at me.

"No, not really, just friends, you know," I said.

I think Sally was getting jealous, being left out of the conversation, so she said, "We don't *really* have to go, do we, J?"

"Yes," I answered, throwing her another warning look. "We really do. We can't leave them waiting there forever, Sally."

Sally just snorted and shrugged, like she had to tolerate me, even though I was a major hindrance to her. She kept glancing down at the cigarette in her hand and had taken all of one puff that I saw. I think she just liked the way it looked in her fingers, the tip glowing in the dark. The only light we had was one pale slice from the hallway and a faded yellow streetlight, spilling down the alley-way. But even in the dim light, I could still make out the gorgeous flashing green of Blue's eyes. I gave Sally a look and motioned for her to hurry up. So Sally started to teeter back down the stairs in her clunky platform sandals. I moved slowly after her, reluctant to leave Blue, his musky wonderful scent, his taut body, and his dangerous eyes. The pull of his current was strong.

"I'm so glad to meet you, Blue," Sally threw up at him in her sing-song voice, as she continued clunking carefully down the steps, gripping tight to the railing with one hand. As I watched her, I was glad I had been smart enough to wear plain white sneakers. "Next time, I hope we can come *inside* to see you." The last part she tossed back sarcastically, in my direction.

"Bye, Sal," said Blue. "You can come on back, anytime."

Once Sally was half-way down, Blue gently reached over and circled my wrist with his fingers, pulling me around to face him. "Hey," he said softly, "good to see you again...Little sister." And there it was, that something pulled taut between us again, so tight I could hardly breathe. His fingers burned on my skin.

"So you really like my music, huh?" he looked at me sideways, almost shyly.

"Yes," I replied, my face and eyes serious. "Oh, yes."

He smiled and gave me a little salute, his other hand still encircling my wrist.

I smiled back and couldn't think of anything else to say that wouldn't sound stupid. I turned to go down the steps, and Blue slowly released his grip. His touch left a warm imprint on my skin. Sally was already at the bottom, looking down at her dwindling cigarette, as if she didn't know quite what to do with it.

When I was half-way down, Blue said, "Hey, Jamie--" I turned to look back up at him. He was standing with his hands propped in his front pockets of his jeans. "Why don't you come back, here...later...after the movies."

I stopped short, my heart suddenly thudding hard.

"Could you do that?" He went on, "--say, around eleven-thirty, when we finish up here?"

"Me? You mean, tonight?" I asked my voice tight in my chest.

He laughed, "Yeah, that's what I meant, later tonight."

"Here?" I asked, pointing to the bottom of the fire-escape.

"Yeah," he said, "there would be good."

"Ok," I found myself saying. All I could think was, *what about Rusty, what about Mom. How can I?* But I couldn't say no. I would have to figure out the details later.

"Kay, see ya." He smiled his sexy smile, gave me a little wave and backed away from the railing until I couldn't see him anymore.

I turned to Sally, who was finally scrunching the cigarette into the gravel with the fat heel of her sandal. She looked at me with her mouth gaping open. I grabbed her by the elbow and hauled her away before she blurted out something stupid that Blue might hear.

CHAPTER SIX

I was still gripping the cap of her sleeve, which had pulled completely off her shoulder by then, when she screeched, "Are you *crazy*? You can't..." She shrugged her shoulder out of my grasp, gave me a scathing look, and readjusted the shirt, puffing the sleeve back up again, perfectly. Bringing her voice down to a hiss she said, "--You *can't* come back. We have to be home in an hour and a half. My Dad's picking us up at the *movies*-- remember?"

"I know, Sal, but--I have to."

"Whoa, Jamie, you could get in BIG trouble for this—I mean, he's totally cute and everything, don't get me wrong—but *this*, well," she gestured wildly, waving her hands dramatically in the air, "this is *dangerous*!" Then she covered her mouth and giggled, giddy and excited that about the idea, "God! What are you gonna do?"

"I'll just have to figure something out." We were striding down the street towards the movie theater across town less than a half-a-mile away, our heads bent together and voices growing tense and hushed, even though there was no one close enough to hear. There were only a few people on the street, a few slow-walking couples holding hands, a pair of guys smoking cigarettes in front of the pool hall—but no one paying any attention to us.

"Jeez, Jamie, those guys are like, *old,* and--I don't know. Maybe I should come with you," she smirked at me, cocking an eyebrow. "You could get into such BIG trouble for this."

"I know, I know, you said that already," I said. "But no, you can't come...besides, two of us missing would be worse. No..." I said, thinking, "I have to go home from the movies like we planned. Then I'll just have to get back out ...once my mom thinks I'm in bed."

"Oh man, I can't believe you. You really think you can get away with *that*? The oldest trick in the book? What if you get caught? Your mother will kill you. And what about getting back in?"

"I don't *know*," I hissed back, getting annoyed with her. I was asking myself the same questions, but I didn't like hearing all the warnings voiced out loud. "I just can't *get* caught."

*   *   *

At eleven-fifteen I sucked in deep breaths of the night air, trying to slow down my pounding heart. I had never been out so late alone, my sneakers padding softly on the cement as I made my escape to the *Apple*. After missing the first twenty minutes of the movie earlier, we had to beg the guy at the movie theatre to let us in to see the rest from the back row. The movie was a love story that took place between a young guy and an older woman on an island off Massachusetts. It was good, but it was hard keeping my mind on the plot when I had my own real life drama reeling through my head. Plus, we missed the whole set-up and all the forbidden kissing only spiked my nerves and imagination about what might happen later that night.

Once Sally's Dad had dropped me "safely" back at home, I slipped like a thief out my first floor bedroom window, just as I planned. I waited until the house was thick with quiet, long after Mom had said good-night, turned out all the lights and brushed her teeth. Each tick between minutes on my clock seemed an eternity. I was terrified of sneaking out, but knew I had to. I couldn't believe I was going to do it, but I couldn't stop myself either. The hardest part was not letting the metal-screen window squeak when I slid it up, then back down. I left it open a couple inches, so I could get back in later without making too much noise.

I walked fast to the *Apple* for the second time that night, afraid to look back, avoiding the harsh glare of the streetlights. I felt exposed in the open circles they cast, jumpy and ill at ease. I couldn't even think about what was going to happen once I got there. So I focused hard on my walking feet, my sneakers slapping softly, one foot, then the other. *Blue,* one foot said, *Blue,* slapped the other.

*   *   *

As I approached the rusty fire-escape stairs, I huffed out a sigh of relief when I saw Blue's motorcycle still chained to the bottom. Then I heard a door *bang*. Followed by voices and a car's idling engine somewhere around the side door. Heart still thudding, I glanced cautiously around the corner of the building. There was a beat-up black van parked in the alley, its doors ajar, with the members of Sunstreak meandering around, carrying their amps and instruments from the back entrance of the *Apple* to the van. Blue stood with a bottle of beer in hand, laughing and talking with them as they loaded their equipment, and my pulse leapt at the sight of him. Just seeing he standing there made my bones go loose and wobbly in my skin. I watched as the sax player held out something to him—Blue put it to his lips and took a long drag, then exhaled a thick plume of bluish smoke. It wasn't just a cigarette, that much I knew.

Their casual attitude, smoking pot so out in the open, worried me. Sure, I had been at parties where a joint was passed around and kids were drinking beer. At those parties, I just said, no thanks, easily, and kept on talking. Here, I felt suddenly out of my depth. What if Blue offered me a hit? Rusty would never let me be around a scene like this. It scared me too, that Blue was getting high when he was supposed to be with me. Rusty's words echoed in my head, *he's into girls, Jamie, and a lot of other stuff too.* Then I was struck by the realization that Blue had asked me back impulsively and without much thought, never expecting that I really would come. I was an idiot. I had risked everything to be there, to see him again. I stood unable to move, mortified, wanting nothing more than to be back in the warm safety of my own bed. But it was too late because Blue's eyes glanced over and caught mine as I hovered in the dim light of the alley. "Well, hey," he said, and a lazy grin spread across his mouth. "Look who's here."

The other guys didn't even seem to notice as they slammed doors shut, slapped Blue on the shoulder and muttered, "Later, man, G'night," and clambered into the van. Their engine revved and the tail-lights flamed red as they backed out past me into the street, and then were gone. Blue held his hand up in casual salute and slid his gaze over to me. "So…C'mon over here, Little Sister." His voice poured down inside me like syrup. I moved slowly toward him, hesitant but hypnotized.

"Well," he said, still smiling down into my face, his hands wedged into his back pockets. "You really came." His eyes were dreamy and glazed-looking, but he was acting normal otherwise.

"Yeah, I'm here," I said, trying to sound calm and sultry. Instead my words came out thin and young-sounding to my ears. But that didn't stop him. He looked down into my eyes. In slow motion, he raised his hand and grazed the back of his knuckles down the skin of my cheek, so lightly, I barely felt it. Yet I shivered.

"You wanna go for a ride?" he asked and dropped his hands casually to the belt loops on either side of my jean-shorts, then tugged me gently toward him. Not close enough to bump up against his hips, but just short of contact. He was so good at this, practiced, I could tell. I could hardly breathe. He smelled musky and smoky and his nearness made me light-headed.

I was scared to go for a ride with him when he had just taken a toke, but I had come all this way. I couldn't back out now. I was stupid under his spell. I would have done almost anything he asked. I gazed back into his eyes and nodded, *yes.*

He took my hand and led me toward the bike, to unchain it. As the chains fell to cement with a clatter, I knew there was no turning back. I wondered vaguely where Blue's guitar was, but realized it was an irrelevant thought. All that mattered was this, *here, now*, climbing onto the back of the motorcycle behind Blue, anticipating the feel of his body pressed up against mine. I didn't even bother to ask where we were going. I was trying to act like none of it mattered and maybe it didn't. Even words seemed inadequate. We had slipped into a dream time, where normal rules didn't apply. Here it was just heat and touch and flowing forward into the night with Blue.

He didn't offer me the extra helmet this time, and I didn't ask, though I had never ridden without one. He wasn't wearing his either; they both remained strapped to the back. My hair felt wispy and loose around my head, my skin exposed. Rusty would have killed me. Blue ignited the engine, checked that my feet were on the pedal sticks, pulled my arms snug around his waist, and we ripped off fast into the night. I leaned up tight against his taut back, intoxicated with his scent and closeness, and we became one.

The streets were quiet, with only a few scattered cars out on the road, and Blue drove with the precision and ease I remembered. His headlights illuminated a thin swath of pavement ahead of us. We were flying through the dark and I just let it all go... fear, expectation—all thoughts of my family. It was just now, and now, and *now*. I knew it was crazy, probably even dangerous, but it was as free as I'd ever felt, as high and giddy and alive, and I wouldn't have given it up for anything in the world. It was as if we'd pushed through a boundary I had always stayed safely behind, and now we were flying out beyond gravity, to a place where we didn't even have to touch the ground. We were heading toward the beach. The night air was cool and humid on my face, skimming across my bare arms and legs. I could hear Blue's music playing in my head. But this time, he was here, *right next to me*.

*   *   *

We pulled into a small sandy parking area, well hidden from the road by a fence of twisted mangrove branches and a cluster of palm trees. There were twelve or thirteen cars and nine or ten motorcycles parked in a haphazard semi-circle. Out of habit, I checked quickly for Rusty's bike or the vehicles of any of his friends.

"Don't worry," Blue said, reading my mind as he kicked down his stand and climbed off the bike. "No big, bad brothers here." He reached for my hand and helped me off too.

"Where are we?" I asked.

"Wonderland…" Blue answered, grinning his sexy grin, pulling my hand around him, looping my arm low around his back, as if we'd been walking together that way forever. I slipped my fingers through his belt loop. He draped his arm over my shoulders. I wanted to stay like that, tucked snug into his side, and walk for miles. Every time he touched me, I felt dizzy. He was leading me out toward the beach, but he probably could have led me anywhere.

"*Really*," I said, a little apprehensive about what lay ahead, though I wanted to seem cool. "What's here?"

"Just some friends of mine," Blue answered. "It's a place we hang out sometimes." Then he stopped, turned his face down to mine. He leaned against me, cupped my chin with his strong fingers and kissed me. His lips were warm and his breath hot, smelling smoky and faintly of beer, and it was a deep searing kiss, hungry. Our bodies melded and I was lost. It was voracious and needy and dizzying, and like no kiss I could ever have imagined. I never wanted it to stop. I was afraid I would sink to my knees, then down to the sand with him, and never come up for air again. So I pulled back, just a little.

"Whoa, "I whispered. I waved my hand in the air as if to disperse its power like smoke.

Blue laughed and pulled me in closer to his chest. "Mmn-nnnm, Jamie." Then he stroked his knuckles down my cheek again, lightly. "My-my, you are dangerous, Little sister…very dangerous. C'mon, party calls."

He took my hand and started leading me down the sandy path in the dark. He clearly knew the way. I could see the glow of a reddish light somewhere ahead and could smell wood smoke in the air.

"Well, I can't stay long," I muttered. But I didn't think Blue even heard me.

The winding path through the sand came out onto a flat stretch of secluded beach. There was a huge driftwood bonfire blazing, its smoke thick in the air, with dark shapes moving in and out of its orange-glow. There must have been at least thirty people scattered throughout the sand, most of them bikers, with a few surfers I recognized too. I prayed none of them knew Rusty. The party had obviously been underway for a while. Some people were sitting on logs, passing joints and drinking from plastic cups. Couples were strewn about on blankets, making singular lumps in the sand, oblivious to their surroundings. Another group of

41

people were dancing to music that poured from a truck parked near the fire, with its doors wide and radio blaring. The truck had a silver keg on its tailgate, which another group of people gathered around, sitting and talking, or standing up inside the truck bed, whooping and laughing loudly. It was a wild crowd and like no party I had ever been to. I was sure a large amount of drugs and beer were being consumed and I thought, *Blue spends a lot of his nights here?*

He squeezed my hand and walked right into the middle of the fray. Everyone seemed to know him. People called to him over the music. "Blue! Hey, man. Blue's here." Guys called and slapped his shoulder, gave him high fives. Three or four girls around the fire smiled at him in a way I didn't like and called in sing-songy voices, "Well, hey, Blue." And I couldn't help but wonder how many of them had been with him. I felt panicked, thinking that Patti might be there too. If she saw me with Blue, I was dead. Not only might she rip my hair out, but even more troubling, she'd tell Rusty where I'd been as well. I walked with my head down uttering a silent prayer to be invisible.

I tripped in the sand and felt suddenly young and stupid, wondering what in the world I was doing there. But Blue caught me, gripped his hand tighter around mine, and then I knew why. Someone handed him a joint and he offered me a drag. I shook my head, no. He took a hit and passed it back, nodding his head to indicate, thanks, no more. We walked back out of the circle of light away from the fire.

"Want a beer?" he asked, as he approached the keg on the truck. Again, I shook my head no, embarrassed. "You sure?" he asked.

"Okay," I answered, thinking *just one won't hurt.*

The crowd in the back of the truck hooted when they saw Blue. "Blue! Hey, it's the guitar man!" One of them shouted. Everyone was teetering around, in there drunkenly. They all laughed and took up the chant "The guitar man...where's your guitar, man? And hey," another shouted, "who's the little guitar girl?" Then finding themselves wildly funny, they dissolved into whoops of laughter. Blue just rolled his eyes, handed me a cup of beer, and then got one for himself. "Y'all are wasted!" he said to them, grinning, and waved them away.

They thought that was hilarious too, and again they hooted and shouted in slurry voices, "Yea, Man, Whooo-eee! Definitely."

Thankfully, Blue motioned for me to follow him off toward the Gulf, where I hoped we would be alone. The party made me nervous. I knew I didn't belong there and as messed up as his friends were, anything could happen. It didn't look like I would be getting home anytime soon either. I knew I was in over my head, way over.

Catcalls from the truck floated in the air behind us. "Bl—ue, Oh Bl—ue, Where ya goin' with the guitar girl, Bluuuuuue?"

Blue must have sensed my unease, because he said, "Sorry darlin', let's go down here and sit for a bit."

He sipped at his beer and I took a bigger gulp of mine than I meant to, trying to calm the twisting ball of nerves in my stomach. We reached a flat dark place in the sand, well away from the noise and hot glow of the fire. Blue sat down and tugged my hand so I would sit too. I sat close-but-not-quite touching his thigh. We both looked up the vast smattering of stars and the thin slice of a crescent moon. There was so much I wanted to say but suddenly, I couldn't find any words.

"Ahhh," Blue said, taking another sip of his beer and lighting a cigarette from his shirt pocket, "Better." Then he twisted his cup down into the sand next to him and I did the same.

"Yeah," I replied. "Much." I began to relax for the first time that night.

"So, little Jamie. I'm truly glad you came," Blue said grinning over at me.

"Me too," I replied, wondering if I really meant it. But looking over at his smile and the gleam of those mesmerizing eyes, even in the pale moonlight, I knew I did.

Blue leaned back onto his elbows and smoked, looking up at the night sky. Then he asked, "You ever think about what's really out there?"

"Oh, yeah," I replied, "all the time."

"—Well, what I think," he went on, "is that it's not magic, really. It's just space. Space and stars and bright planets going on forever. Not that that isn't cool. But whatever people want it to be, need it to be, that's what they look up and make it. Some people call it God, some people see stars. You know?"

"I think so…." I answered. "You mean, we put our wishes up there."

"Our wishes," he echoed. "Exactly."

I felt so close to him then, even closer than when we had kissed. Because this was exactly what I had dreamed of, to be with Blue, to be noticed by him, sitting alone in a beautiful place like this, getting inside his head. Hearing his thoughts out loud. I could scarcely believe it was real; I had fantasized a scene just like it in my mind so many times since I had first seen him. So I sent my own silent thank you up to the stars.

"So," I asked, "What's your wish?"

"My wish," he hesitated. "Well, I hope someday my music will mean something to people—people outside of Taraberg, Florida, that is."

I looked up at the stars and pointed to one. "Wish granted," I said.

He laughed. "Wow, can you really do that? Grant wishes?"

"Well, maybe I can." I grinned over at him, feeling relaxed enough now to be playful, even a little flirtatious. "Really, though," I said, "your music *is really* something already, Blue. It's going to take you places far away from here. I don't think you need the stars to make that one come true."

"Hope so...some fricking day, if I ever get out of here," he murmured. "Thanks for doing that, though, with the star. Who knows, maybe it'll do the trick."

He reached over and ran his fingers gently over my face and lips, tracing it like a blind man, memorizing, and I shivered again. He leaned over to kiss me. We kissed and kissed, then melted down into the ground somehow, and I didn't even care that I was getting sand in my hair and in my clothes. We lay with our limbs entwined, rolling together, and he kissed me and kissed me until I thought I would die. Our mouths and bodies hungry for each other, tongues searching and needing more and more, until I lost track of anything but his taste, his scent, the feel of his fingers in my hair, on the bare skin of my lower back where my shirt was pulled up. I knew I was slipping over a steep cliff now, because if he kept on, there was no getting back to the edge. "Blue," I murmured, reluctantly, "Blue, it's getting late..."

"Oh," he groaned, rolling away slowly to his back, "Whoa, Baby."

I loved the words he said, and the way he said them. I loved his feel and his kiss. But I knew I was moving into a place I didn't know how to get back from. "I'm sorry," I said, "really."

"Oh, hey...it's okay," he replied, letting out a huge breath and running his sexy hand over his chest. "Whoa. I better watch myself here. You make me forget whose little sister you are."

I was both thrilled and irritated by his words. Pleased that I knew he was as sucked into this vortex as I was and irritated because there was the age thing again, and Rusty. It was the first time in my life I really wished I had no brother at all. But I also knew I had to get home. Like Cinderella, I felt my time running dangerously out.

"Just give me a minute, here," he said. We finally collected ourselves, brushed off the sand and wandered back toward the light of the party in silence. Once I had my head together a bit, I remembered one of the things I wanted to ask him.

"Blue," I asked, "how did you get that name?"

"My old man," he replied, "he told my mom to call me Brendan, but he left my mom a long time ago. She was only seventeen when she got pregnant. He never married her and finally just split. Funny thing, she won't tell me who he was, but she hinted that he was a musician. So I guess I got the genes. She says my first word was 'boo' or 'blue' or something like that. She used to be an artist, so I guess she decided it some kind of miracle my first word was a color. But I think maybe she just didn't want to call me something he named me. My mom's kind of a dreamer," I sensed a deep sadness when he spoke of his mother, "or she used to be."

"Brendan Reed," I murmured. So that's your real name. Blue's much better, suits you," I said. "Have you ever heard of Picasso?"

"You know about him?" Blue asked, excitement creeping back into his voice. "Hell, yeah, my mom showed me a book of his work once, and she used to take me to museums, teaching me all about art. Picasso's Blue period, that weird guy playing the blue guitar, you know that? Wow. I never met anyone who knows about that. So, you're cute *and smart*." He took my hand and grinned down at me.

I bumped hard against his shoulder. "Funny," I said, "real funny, *Brendan*."

He laughed and we walked back slowly and I was less afraid. I didn't want to hope too much, or jinx it, but I felt something pulled tighter between us now. That initial spark had melded into something stronger, there was something real between us now. I could walk by the fire and all those staring faces and know that it had been me out here with Blue, listening to his secrets. Not Patti, not one of those other girls, just me, Jamie.

One of my favorite songs was pouring from the truck radio as we wandered back. Most of the partiers were sitting down now, talking on the tailgate. The mood seemed to have mellowed some. They were still drunk, but now beyond rowdy. One of them seemed to be asleep, passed out in the truck bed. I heard the heart-tugging opening strains of the notes to "Stairway to Heaven."

And again, as if reading my mind, Blue just swept me up close and we started to dance across the sand. I loved the silky feel of it under my bare feet. The slow part of the song began to build, and I closed my eyes and clung to him, his smell, his blond curls ruffling near my cheek, and the strong taut feel of his lean body next to mine. We fit just right. We danced slow and close until the fast part of the song, and then he whirled me around, lifting me right up off the ground, and we laughed, lost in each other and in the electric pulse of the music. He spun me in and back out. Then as the song slowed again toward the end, we drifted back close together, breathing hard, and lingered until the last note. I knew the drunks on the truck were watching us, but they seemed momentarily rendered speechless. When we finished, they started clapping and hooting again.

Blue just grinned and waved, bowed, grabbed my hand, and pulled me back towards his motorcycle and the dark path.

We were quiet for the whole ride back to my house, draped in a kind of closeness beyond words. I held my arms around Blue's waist and leaned up against him. I took in the rushing cool night air all around us, and I thought *no matter what happens now, at least I know how this feels. At least I had this.*

He dropped me on a corner a block from my house. He kissed me once, tenderly, his lips lingering and squeezed my hand. Then he sped off into the night. I watched him go, felt him slipping further and further away from me. I touched my fingertips to my lips, feeling the heat left by his kiss. He left me with no promise of seeing him again. But I was sure that after tonight, how could we not? Everything on my street looked new and different. I walked home admiring the beauty everywhere and slid back through my window and into bed. It was one-forty-five in the morning, but I still couldn't fall asleep. I was too jazzed up and weak with relief that apparently my mother hadn't noticed that I was ever gone.

CHAPTER SEVEN

In the morning, I had to face my mother. I shuffled tentatively toward the kitchen, hoping the window hadn't screeched too loud, praying that the changes last night had brought over me wouldn't show. I stood with the refrigerator door propped open and poured a glass or orange juice, just as I had hundreds of mornings before. Mom was sitting at the kitchen counter clutching her coffee mug, watching me. "Door," she reminded me, and as usual, I shut it and this scene had been replayed morning after morning. I was trying to make everything seem as normal as possible.

"Sorry, mom," I muttered, keeping my voice as calm and sleepy as I could. I sat on the stool next to her at the counter. "Guess we're eating in here, today."

"Morning, Hon," she replied, still watching me over her coffee cup as I sat down. "Yeah, I was too tired to walk out to the lanai."

I fought the blush that was threatening to rise to my face under her scrutiny. Though I was trying to be my old self, part of me was still floating, detached, on the beach dancing in the dark with Blue.

"Did you hear anything funny last night?" Mom asked, and my heart started pounding.

"Funny?" I asked, taking a quick gulp of orange juice—petrified, but still trying to seem calm and appropriately confused.

"Well, I don't' know, but I thought I heard someone up late last night," she shook her head. "It wasn't you?" she studied me with those smoky eyes, searching for cracks, I knew.

"Don't think so…no," I replied, "I got up to go to the bathroom, I think. I must have been half asleep. I hardly remember." I shrugged, thinking, *don't blab so much, just cool it, keep your mouth shut.*

"Huh," she went on. "Well, I thought maybe it was Rusty coming in late or something. Guess not."

I finished my juice and got up to make some toast, sure my nerves would prevent me from actually eating it. But at least it got me away from those eyes. I needed to get out of there before something gave me away. She was too good at reading me. Maybe it was a perfect time to go clean Skipper's cage.

"So, what are you up to today?" she asked, thankfully taking the pressure off. "You're still planning on helping with the Pier Fourth stuff, aren't you?"

I had almost forgotten. Every Fourth of July, Taraberg had a family festival in the park next to the waterfront pier and fireworks over the water at night. Dad and the Taraberg Lions' Club had been the ones to organize the town years ago into doing it. It was a week–and-a-half away now. Mom was always an honorary committee member, and Sally I were traditionally roped into assisting with the bike parade, rides, dunking booth and other kids' activities—basically, anything the adults in charge ordered us to do. Practically everyone in Taraberg came to the fireworks. I hoped that Blue wouldn't be one of them. The thought of him seeing me in the red and white striped apron spinning a number wheel or something else equally stupid was mortifying. But what else was there to do in Taraberg? "Yeah, Mom, course I'm helping," I replied. "What do you need?"

*   *   *

After a week of set-up and preparation, another Fourth was dawning. While the sun was still high and the heat just beginning to bear down, we were busy making last minute adjustments. Blue still hadn't called me. I had a thin worm of worry twisting around in my stomach, but I was trying to ignore it. *It's only been a week,* I kept telling myself.

The festival was kicking off in less than two hours with a kids' bike parade at noon. Mom, Sally and I and about fifteen other women and men from the town committee had laced strings of Japanese lanterns around the booths and bandstand, and red and white and blue banners on the gates around the park. The lanterns would be illuminated later, at dusk. The men on the committee had assembled rows of white painted booths where the games were run: a roulette wheel, a dart balloon game, a golf putting game, and more. Clusters of red, white and blue balloons, which we had tediously filled with helium and tied to ribbons, flew from the booths and any available post we could find. The carnival people had arrived two days earlier to set up the old hand-painted carousel, Ferris wheel, and the mini-roller coaster we rented every year. There were a bit old and shabby, but they were all we could afford and part of the Taraberg Fourth tradition. They sat empty, but now ready for people.

The guys from the famous Orlando Fireworks Company had also been working for days setting up the display on the old flat barge anchored in the harbor. Later, everyone would spread blankets and lawn chairs near the pier to watch the pyrotechnics. Everything looked great. As much as I moaned about all the work, I really didn't mind bringing the Taraberg Fourth to life every year. It felt like paying tribute to Dad, it had meant so much to him. I knew it was like that for Mom too. Even though we never said it out loud, it was a way of keeping alive his memory and we always felt his presence there. There was something to be said for traditions, they held people together somehow. Rusty was still at the shop, but even he always made an effort to come by and grill hamburgers and hotdogs to sell at the food court for a few hours. That was his contribution.

Mom told Sally and me to take a break, so we decided to get a cold drink. At the booth, Mr. Everly kidded us about how tall we'd gotten, same as always, and poured us huge cups of lemonade from the bulbous glass machine that made it. Gallons of lemonade swirled around inside it, with a tropical fruit punch machine right beside it.

"I don't know, Jamie," he blustered, "you're looking more like your Mama everyday. Pretty as a picture, I'd say." Mr. Everly always talked loud and laughed a lot, with his taut round belly bouncing up under his shirt. We liked him. We went to school with his son Michael.

"Thanks, Mr. Everly," I replied.

"Anytime, anytime. You girls get thirsty, just c'mon back, we'll take care of ya here. On the house, on the house-" he waved away our money.

"Thanks, Mr. Everly," Sally said, batting her eyes innocently at him. We made our way over to a picnic table and sat down. "Whew," Sally said, waving her hand to her face like a fan. "Your mom is a slave driver."

"Tell me about it, "I replied. "And the day's only begun."

"We have to work the carousel *and* the bike parade?" Sally whined.

"Yeah, we've got the first two hour shift on the carousel, and the bike parade's easy and over early, after that we should be able to walk around, see who's here. We're off duty for the fireworks, and that's the best part anyway."

"I am NOT coming back for clean-up tomorrow morning," Sally insisted. "I have a date for the fireworks tonight and I will probably be up *late,* so I am not getting up at the crack of dawn again."

"I know, Sal, you told me already, about twelve times. Eight AM is not the crack of dawn, but I hear ya. The maintenance guys help with that part anyway, so there'll be enough other people doing it."

"Tell me again why we do this every year?" Sally whined.

"Tradition!" I answered, tapping a toast against her lemonade cup and taking a huge gulp of my own.

"You think Blue will come?" Sally asked, sliding a glance over at me. She took a delicate sip of her drink.

Just the mention on his name made my heart lurch and my face grow hotter than it already was. "I don't know," I answered, shrugging, acting like I couldn't care less.

"He *still* hasn't called you?"

I shook my head no.

"Jamie, it's been a *week*!"

"I'm aware of that, Sal."

"Well, I would kill him, if that were me, I would. You're really *so* lucky you didn't get caught sneaking out like that."

"Uh-uh," I answered, ignoring her as best I could. "So, who is *your* hot date tonight?" I asked, changing the subject fast.

"Walter Harvey," she said, grinning wickedly.

"Walt Harvey? The *senior*?" I asked. "*Mr. Basketball?*"

"Yup-" answered Sally, looking smug.

"How did you pull that off?"

Then she launched into a long-winded story about how somebody knew Walter's younger sister, and Sally hinted around about wanting to go out with him, was he interested, and about word traveling through an elaborate grapevine of people, which resulted in Sally's big date. Only Sally could finagle a date with Walter Harvey, one of the tallest and best-looking jocks at Taraberg High. It was a perfect match, I was sure. And at least it had gotten her off the subject of Blue.

*   *   *

The bike parade around the paved pathways of the park had been a success. There were twenty-five kids or more with decorated bikes, babies in wagons and people with dogs wearing red, white and blue bandanas in a long, meandering line. Considering the chaos, it had been fun, and there were no major injuries—except one scraped knee that Mom fixed with a band-aid.

A few hundred people were now wandering around the park, kids lined up at the game booths, some eating snow cones, and adults visiting and trying to ignore the ninety-five degree heat. For two hours Sally, Mr. Everly's son Michael, and I had been lifting kids on and off the carousel horses, collecting tickets, and stopping and starting the ride. I found myself searching through the crowd all day, hoping for a glimpse of Blue. Yet I was dreading the possibility of him seeing me doing something so stupid and uncool. I was dripping in the heat. My red tank top was blotched with dark spots and my arms ached. The tinny repetitious carousel music and squealing kids were starting to give me a headache. I was relieved when two other kids we knew came to take our place, our shift over at last.

"Thank God," Sally muttered. "I've gotta go to the ladies' room, I need to change this shirt before Walter sees me."

She looked perfectly cool and crisp to me, in her skimpy white midriff baring shirt and khaki shorts. Sally never seemed to look disheveled. In the humidity, my hair was frizzing out in wild curls around my head. Hers looked freshly brushed, blonde smooth ripples flowing down her back. I was sure Walter, or any other guy within fifty miles, would not mind one bit the way she looked. Michael had been practically drooling. Sometimes, I hated Sally. We rushed to the brick building where the restrooms were, and then had to wait five minutes in line to get inside the ladies' room.

We had both brought a change of clothes, deodorant, perfume and make-up in our backpacks. It took me a few minutes to get changed and cleaned up, while it took Sally at least twenty-five. Everyone in there was giving us dirty looks for taking up the sink space so long, but Sally didn't seem to notice. I thought she looked fine to begin with. At least the bathroom was cool. Finally, we were ready to head back to the heat and the crowds.

"Okay," Sally said, striding along through the people like they weren't even there, "here's the plan. I'm looking for Walter and anybody else good we know, and you look around for Blue. We'll meet up back by the drink booth in fifteen, twenty-minutes—got it?"

"Kay," I nodded, even though I had a sinking feeling Blue was nowhere to be found. Not there, anyway. Blue was not the family-festival type. More the type to show up late, maybe, for the fireworks. I just hoped he wasn't playing at the *Apple* that night.

*   *   *

Sally found Walter and a bunch of his friends wandering around. Now they were all riding the roller coaster for the third time. I stood leaning against the flimsy metal rail watching them scream and throw up their hands, even though this roller coaster was practically a kid ride. I had already been on it twice, and the thrill was gone for me. I felt awkward around Walter and his friends anyway, mostly seniors and their girlfriends. I guessed I wasn't trying that hard to fit in either. I just wanted to see Blue. It was funny, because these were the really "cool"

51

kids at our school, and a few weeks ago, I probably would have been thrilled for a chance to hang out with them. Now, they seemed young to me and, honestly, kind of boring. So I was keeping to myself a bit and not saying much.

Where was Blue? I wondered, for the hundredth time that day. I kept imagining that I saw his face in the crowd.

I had promised my mother that I would meet Rusty, Shelly, and her for our annual picnic dinner. Then she said we could go off with our own friends for the fireworks afterward. I checked my watch and it was almost 7:00, time to head back. When Sally got off, I told her I was going to meet Mom for supper.

"So, catch y'all later, then. Nice to meet you." I waved and started to walk away. Sally was putting all her efforts into flirting with Walter, and it looked like it was working. He seemed to have a perpetual smirk on his face and he couldn't keep his hands off her. They hardly noticed I was leaving.

"Wait!" Sally called, disentangling herself to run after me. She grabbed my elbows and whispered intensely into my face. "J—we'll meet you at the gate behind the bandstand at 8:00. Don't be late. I think Walter and the guys want to party before the fireworks, you know, maybe smoke and drink a little, if you catch my drift. God, isn't he just *so* cute?" I could tell by the way her eyes were flashing that Sally thought it was the best thing in the world to be invited to "party" with the seniors.

"Absolutely," I answered. "Kay, catch you later. Have fun, Sal, and try to stay out of *trouble.*"

Sally romped back to Walter's many arms. He took up where he left off, all over her in a matter of minutes.

Sure, I thought. Sally and trouble belonged together. She always seemed to get away with it though, somehow. I meandered back toward the picnic tables.

It was still bright out, but the sun was sinking lower, casting everything in a soft golden light. It was my favorite time of summer, the beginning of twilight. It had always seemed magical to me, fairy light. People were still walking around the park, though the pace had slowed. Many of them were spreading blankets and chairs in the grass, saving a place for the fireworks, while enjoying picnics and taking in the sunset.

Just as I saw Mom and Shelly spreading a paisley cloth over a picnic table, I caught a glimpse of Rusty at the edge of the park near the road. He was standing next to a circle of motorcycles parked under the trees, talking to a group of his friends. I looked over them each carefully, feeling my heart begin to pound. They were close enough that I could see their faces clearly: One of them was Blue.

He was sitting casually astride his bike, wearing his faded jeans and his green tee-shirt. I saw clearly who was sitting right behind him too. The long dark hair was unmistakable, the thin arm draped possessively around his neck. My stomach swelled with nausea. I felt hot spit rising in the back of my throat, sour lemonade. I wanted to run, scream, anything, but Mom and Shelly had already seen me approaching. I stood paralyzed, unable to move, either forward or back, my eyes fixed on Blue.

I watched in horrified silence as Patti leaned down to nuzzle her face against Blue's cheek, watched as he tilted his face up to brush her with a kiss. A quick, over-the-shoulder kiss, then he turned back to Rusty. Patti pulled up to standing, swung her black hair like a scarf over her shoulder, then her leg, standing beside him, leaning over him. He must have seen me, standing there in the middle of the sidewalk, alone, only fifty feet away. Yet he had kissed her as if it were the most natural thing in the world. As if that night with me, just one week ago, had meant nothing, had never even happened. *Patti?* I thought, *no.* And I felt like an artery burst, gushing blood hot as a flame, but deep inside me, where no one could see. I forced myself to turn away, sleep-walked to the table, saw my mother's lips move, but I couldn't hear what she was saying. *How will I eat?* I thought. *I won't be able to eat now.*

"Jamie? *Hello*," Mom said, her face coming into focus. "Where on earth are you? Did you have fun?"

"Oh yeah, I'm here…" I replied, my voice faint. I was trying to keep her face in focus, concentrating on not looking back over to that circle of motorcycles at the edge of the road. Anywhere but there.

"Hey, J!" Shelly said, giving me a smile, "How you doin', kiddo?"

"Fine," I answered, still feeling weak. She seemed to be looking at me oddly, but she said nothing.

We emptied the coolers and spread the food Mom had prepared on the tablecloth: potato salad, grilled chicken, a fat cluster of green grapes, a jug of iced tea, a home-made blueberry pie. Shelly and Mom chatted comfortably, but I could find no words. I couldn't find my voice. It had sunk deep inside me, disappeared like a pebble down a well. It was there on the bottom somewhere underwater, small and far away. So I listened and nodded and acted like I heard every word they said, though sounds were muted.

Rusty wandered back over to our table and I managed to mutter, "Hi," to his hearty, "Hey, J," but it was all I could get out. I didn't even look up at him because I knew Rusty would have seen it in my eyes. And I couldn't look to the road either, so I wouldn't look up at all. Instead, I uncharacteristically helped set the table with great care, my head bent over, concentrating on the mundane: silverware, paper plates, red napkins. *That's it,* I thought, *don't think.* Around me, the world kept spinning. Rusty and Mom and Shelly filled up their plates with the food and chatted amiably, while I tried to hold on.

CHAPTER EIGHT

I don't know how I got through dinner. I saw myself, almost from the outside, listening, moving, pushing food around on a paper plate. Pretending to take bites, though the food was dirt in my mouth. But on the inside, the artery kept quietly leaking, burning at my stomach and aching in my heart.

Still in a daze, I said good-bye, promised Mom I'd meet her later and drifted off to meet Sally. The lanterns around the park had been lit and now glowed, white stars softened by their paper covers. Kids darted around holding sparklers, drawing dizzy circles and letters in the air, until they fizzled out. Then they ran back to their parents for more. It had become clear night, the heat and humidity fading a little with the dusk. It was a perfect night for the fireworks, except for the mosquitoes.

I didn't want to find Sally. What I wanted was to go home and fall into bed, into the painless oblivion of sleep. I wanted to go somewhere where I didn't have to carry around the weight of my body or feel the pressure of my heart beating in my chest. I wondered if it would ever go away now that I had it, or would it become a permanent pain, like a limp, as if I had always walked that way.

I tried and tried to make sense of it. The details spun over and over in my mind: our motorcycle rides, his hands moving over the hollow of my lower back, his lips and fingers tracing my face, his voice and hair in the wash of the spotlight, his eyes, the steps we danced in the sand. Then tonight, seeing him perched on his bike, *Patti behind him, leaning down...*I blotted it out, not wanting to see it all over again, feeling sick. How could he just...

"--Jamie!" I was jolted to the present by Sally's familiar squeal. "J— over HERE!"

"We're over *here!*" she yelled again. I saw her moving amidst the small herd of seniors by the park gate. I dreaded joining them, but where else would I go? I almost turned and walked away, not even answering her call. But as I hesitantly approached them, Sally grabbed, pulling me hard by the wrist. *"Come on,"* she said, "what's *wrong* with you? We're leaving."

I didn't ask where we were going. I didn't care. I just followed, as Sally yanked me along the road. Walter and his friends strolled beside us on lanky legs, talking and laughing, hands shoved into their shorts' pockets. The road we walked was closed off for the fireworks. I could tell we were headed for the baseball field. The "dugout" was well known, hidden from the road, and just remote enough to be a popular place for kids to sit and party undetected. A couple of the boys slunk off to their cars, returning to our parade brazenly carrying six-packs. We all streamed into the dugout and huddled around on the narrow benches. It smelled musty and damp down inside, like mildewed clothes and sweat. Several guys rolled joints from bags of pot they seemed to have pulled from nowhere. Cans of beer were snapped open, passed around, as were two pint bottles of vodka. Lighters were flicked, joints lit. The air was filled with the thick, sweet-scented smoke of pot, making me nauseous and the patter of voices. Walter took a beer can with one hand and then put his other arm around Sally.

I was next to Sally on the bench, then a junior named Jessica was next to me. She jerked her body around, babbling and leaning first into the girl on her right, then back towards me, bobbing around annoyingly. I wanted to smack her. It was too close and crowded, and I waved away a joint as it was passed by. They were all just dark shapes around me, blabbing, telling stories and jokes, giggling, flirting. I sat silent, until Jessica handed me the pint of vodka. I took it and swallowed four disgusting gulps. It burned all the way down, but that didn't stop me.

"*God!*" Jessica gasped.

"Jamie!" Sally admonished, pulled away from Walter by the tone of Jessica's voice. "What the hell are you doing?"

"Drinking," I replied, deadpan. Everyone laughed. Sally gave me a warning look, but kept quiet.

"Hey, there," one of the guys said, handing me a beer "Try this on for size, Slugger."

I took the can and inhaled some huge gulps, two, three, four…then tipped it back down. It tasted harsh and acrid after the vodka, burning the back of my throat. But at least it was cold. They all laughed, amazed at my feat. "Whoa! D'see that? *Yeah*, she's a slugger all right!" The guys marveled. And that became my nickname for the night.

They smoked and drank and the laughter grew louder, the talk more raucous. I sat back against the dugout wall, silent and alone in the crowd. I felt my body grow first light and tingly, then thick, heavy and slow.

By the time we stumbled out of the dugout, maybe one or two kids were still sober. The earth felt spongy and unpredictable under the soles of my sneakers, with odd rolls in it, especially in the full darkness. I tripped going over a curb and giggled, "Whoops."

Sally, still only mildly buzzed, glared at me from under Walter's arm. "God, Jamie," she hissed, "you're wasted."

"Oh well," I muttered, "What're-you-gonna do?" I giggled again, as the words somehow mushed together in my mouth.

"I'll tell you what your mother is going to do," she hissed again, "You damn well better sober up before you see *her* again, or Rusty, jeezus, he'll *kill* you."

"No prob--" I replied, waving my hand in the air. "S-ss, no problem a-tall," though in the foggy back of my mind, I knew it might be a problem after all. The thing was, I could still see Blue's face in the back of my mind too, leaning up to kiss Patti's cheek. Suddenly, all I wanted to do was sit down on the pavement and sob.

"Oh, leave her alone," Walter said. "She'll be fine, once the fireworks are over. It'll wear off. Besides, she's funny like this. Just having a good time, right Jamie?" He grinned, his face looking huge and looming to me, as he slapped my back jovially.

"Abso—luly," I replied. "*Great* time." And he laughed, though Sally clucked her tongue in disgust. "It's not funny," I heard her mutter to him. He just pulled into his side with his long arm and said, "Oh, babe..." The others walked around me, talking, laughing even more loudly than before. "YAH! WOO-WOO!" One of the boys shouted, "Time for the *frigging fireworks!*"

"YEAH! LET'S GO-DO-THE-FIREWORKS!" another boy chanted back. Then I remembered why I hated crowds, because they became these brainless moving blobs like this one was becoming. They were dark shadow figures around me, and I could not make out their faces or determine who was who. The pace quickened and by some silent agreement, everyone surged in together, almost running, while I fell to the back of the pack. I couldn't seem to make my feet move smoothly— too heavy—and I began to fall farther behind.

"Wait up!" I called, but they were all moving away fast into the darkness. Not even Sally seemed to notice that I was being abandoned by the mob. But after a moment, I didn't care. People were idiots anyway. Suddenly, nothing seemed funny anymore, only melancholy and tragic. I plopped down clumsily under the nearest tree, bereft and heartsick.

I looked up, heard the familiar whine and pop--saw the first blood-red explosion burst in the air above me and scatter into sparks. *Beautiful,* I thought. A moment later my stomach lurched into a fist and I was heaving into the grass. Everything came gushing out in a hot liquid rush.

Once the heaving stopped, a sob leaked out, and more followed, until my shoulders were racked and sore and my throat felt raw. I finally gasped for air, tasting vomit and tears, hearing the cracks of fireworks above me. Finally empty and sober, I wiped my face and mouth as best I could. I moved from the putrid mess I'd made to a new spot of prickly clean grass farther away. Sitting alone, I looked up to the wondrous bursts of color exploding into the sky and thought, *Dad. Oh Dad, I'm so sorry.*

CHAPTER NINE

The remnants of my Fourth of July night the next morning were a throbbing in my head and a cold clamp of ache around my heart. Every time I thought of Blue, it squeezed tighter. I wished I didn't have to be conscious, ever again. I closed my eyes again, trying to shut it all out. I could tell from the way the light was angling into my room that it was late. I was surprised Mom hadn't woken me. She was always one of those don't-waste-the-day types. She looked at me funny when I straggled back to the picnic table last night after the fireworks and asked if I was all right. I answered "Fine," and we rode home in silence. I hoped I didn't smell bad. Though I could feel her glancing worriedly over from time to time, thank God, she asked me no questions.

I slumped over my cereal bowl in the lanai trying to forget everything, while Skipper-dee chirruped at me cheerfully from his white hanging cage. I contemplated covering him up, as I was in no mood for his perkiness. But I couldn't, he was just too happy to see me. He flew over and landed on the top of my head, then jumped down and started pecking at a couple of cheerios I put on the table for him. I squinted in the harsh light to read the note on the table Mom had left, saying she was doing errands and would be back by eleven, so at least I had some peace and solitude. Then the phone jangled fiercely into the quiet, making my head pound. I hesitated, but finally shuffled over to pick it up on the third ring. The rooster clock on the kitchen wall read ten-fifteen.

"L'o," I mumbled, through my mouthful of cheerios.

"What the hell *happened* to you, last night, J? Where did you *go*? We were looking for you everywhere--" It was too early for me to respond to Sally's rapid-fire interrogation. So I stayed silent until she calmed down.

"*Jamie*...are you there?"

"Yeah, I'm here, Sal. And I was there last night too, until you dumped me in the park."

"*Dumped* you? *Dumped* you! I looked for you for a half-hour after you *disappeared, J.* You could have at least told me where Miss Loner was taking off to this time…we were all looking for you. We missed half the fireworks because of you --"

"Yeah, I'll bet, for maybe, five minutes, before Walter put his hands all over you again and you forgot—'Ooh, Mr. Octopus.'"

"--*Jamie*! That is a totally crappy thing to say, and you know it. I am NOT even going to talk you about this anymore. Obviously, you found your way home. Good. *Drunk* as you were, I had no idea what might have happened to you."

"Yea, Look, Sal, I'm…sorry. I'm just tired and I have a very bad headache. I was stupid about the drinking thing, you're right, and I am paying for it, believe me. But I can't talk right now. Last night was just… awful. And I can't--Can I just talk to you about it later?"

"Oh, *fine*," Sally backed down, too. "I'm sorry we lost you, but we really did try to find you again."

"I know, I believe you. Thanks. And I'm really glad the thing worked out with Walter."

"Yea, it *really* did. He is such a *sweetie*, isn't he?" She was revived again, and I was sure she would love to go on about Walter for hours, but I didn't have the heart for it.

"He is. Definitely. So, I'll talk to you later, then, 'kay? Bye for now," I said, hurrying her up.

"Bye J, but you gotta tell me what happened later. Promise?"

"Promise."

"Good, Kay. Bye then!" And Sally hung up, ready, I was sure to go call somebody else who would listen as she went raving on and on about Walter Harvey. I sat back down to finish my cheerios and try to get motivated to go cut my Saturday lawns, with my pounding head and my heart squeezed so tight, I could hardly breathe.

*   *   *

It was so dumb. Maybe if I hadn't been so tired and hung-over, it would never have happened. I was cutting the Morrisey's lawn.

60

They have a bank that slopes down to a pond in the backyard, and I lost my footing. The grass was slick from the sprinklers they had on earlier. Whatever the reason, I slid, and my left foot disappeared underneath the mower. It took only a second, as I looked down horrified, there was a sickening crunch as the blade caught. I let go of the handle. The mower drifted slowly down toward the pond, as I sank back onto my butt in the grass clutching my mangled toes and sneakers, which were quickly blotching with red. I felt nothing at first, just shock and surprise, and then the pain started pooling in, hot and vicious. I started screaming, "Ahh, Ahh!" The next thing I knew, Mrs. Morrisey was next to me.

"It's okay, Jamie, it's going to be okay?" But I could see that her face was pasty and her eyes dark with worry. Her hands were shaking as she pressed a clean dishtowel to my foot, "Thank God I was home. I saw it from the window. I've called the ambulance. They're on their way." She was trying to keep her voice neutral and calm, I could tell.

Her six year-old, Brian, looked on and said, "Icky..." I was still moaning, "Ahhh, ahhh, ahhh." The once-white sneaker of my left foot was now soaked through and stained bright red. Blood was oozing out between my fingers and leaking through the towel fast.

"It's going to be okay," Mrs. Morrisey repeated like a mantra, trying to calm herself as much as me, I could tell. "Brian, you go on back to the house, now, honey, and wait until the ambulance man comes. Then, can you bring him right where we are?"

"'Mm-Kay," Brian muttered and shuffled back toward the house. Over his shoulder he said, "Can I ride in it? The amboolance?"

"Not now, honey," Mrs. Morrisey replied.

"Oh miGod, miGod," I mumbled. "ARE THEY STILL THERE? ARE THEY STILL THERE?" And I started searching through the grass for my toes, horrified they might really be there, separate from my body. I was getting a little out of my head by then.

"No, I don't' think so," Mr. Morrisey said, none to convincingly, and she glanced around a bit too, which naturally only intensified my panic. The pain was red-hot and I wanted to scream, but I gritted my teeth together, trying to hold it in.

The next thing I remembered was being in the hospital. I had a vague memory of a cute ambulance attendant who loaded me onto the stretcher. I think I was cracking jokes at him. He probably thought I was nuts. Except maybe they were used to people acting crazy when they were wounded, maybe lots of people flipped out and told dumb jokes in ambulances, for all I knew. It was my first time. He kept asking me slow questions, as if I were deaf, about my address and what my name was. I guess he was checking to see just how out of it I really was. I remember I screamed when they tried to peel off what was left of my sneaker to have a look.

"Are they gone?" I screamed. "Are they gone?"

He shook his head of shaggy brown hair, "No, no, nothing's gone. All still there, just a little cut up, but you're going to be fine." Except whatever they were doing down there hurt like hell. I tried not to scream.

A little cut up could mean a lot of things. *Or was he just trying to calm me down?* I wondered. *Would I ever walk again?* Insane thoughts kept zipping through my mind, and then I would fade out. Everything was in and out of focus, snippets of memories, until the stiff white sheets of the hospital bed where I now lay. I did vaguely remember the doctor examining and then stitching my foot, and other people rushing around, nurses asking more questions. They gave me a shot that made everything afterwards far away and hard to remember. Now I was dying of thirst. My foot was throbbing, wrapped and propped up on a pillow mysteriously, so I had no idea of the extent of the damage. Everything was still and quiet in the room, the bed next to me empty. What I wanted most was my mother. Where was she? Hadn't they called her by now?

Then the most startling thing happened. A woman in a wheelchair was pushed in toward the bed next to me. She had her hand wrapped in gauze and her shoulder-length dark hair fell across her eyes, hiding half her face. The nurse brought her over to the bed and asked if she wanted to lie down. She murmured "No, no thank you," so quietly I could hardly hear her soft voice. "I'll just stay here," she whispered. And the nurse left her in the chair, replying, "If you need help or want anything, just press here," and showed her the call button. The woman nodded.

"May I have some water, please?" I asked the nurse, as she bustled out of the room. I really wanted to ask about my mother, but I figured I would do it when she came back with my water.

"'Kay, honey, on its way," the nurse replied. "And your mom should be here any minute," then she left.

I looked over at the woman, trying to meet her eyes, to maybe say hello, but she was gazing dully out the second-story window to the hospital parking lot below. There was something achingly sad about her and something familiar. I was trying to remember where I might have seen her before. She was only in her late thirties, early forties, about my mom's age, but her thin face looked drawn. I could see that she used to be pretty, but now looked prematurely old. She looked very thin and fragile.

"Nice view," I said, trying to break the silence. But she didn't respond, just kept gazing down toward the parking lot. She seemed to have a delayed reaction, because she brushed the hair gingerly off her cheek and looked over at me out of the corner of her eye, seconds after I spoke. I sucked in my breath at the sight of her face. A huge yellow, grey, and purple bruise covered her swollen cheek and circled her left eye, now exposed by her brushed back hair. Her eyes were dark and filled with something so deep and haunting, it seared my heart. She looked away again and I felt bad for embarrassing her. I knew her face must hurt, and her hand too, whatever those bandages were hiding, but she showed no signs of pain. She looked like she was only half-alive.

"I-" but my words drifted off. I had no idea what to say.

And then, Blue came striding through the door, walking fast, his face set and grim. I had a moment of sheer delight when I thought, *Oh man, am I dreaming? He's come to save me. How could he have known?* Suddenly I remembered how awful I must look, with my hair all smashed down on one side, my face pale, and my foot propped up like a giant torpedo. And also, I was still mad about what he did last night. Then I caught myself and realized Blue hadn't even seen me. I knew then why the woman looked so familiar, though he was blond, and she dark, they looked so much alike. He strode angrily right past me, unseeing, over to the woman. He knelt down in front of her swiftly, saying, "Dammit, oh dammit, Mom. Let me see...." He put his hand gently on top of hers. Then he brushed her hair so tenderly back from her cheek it made me ache, and their conversation was so intimate, it felt wrong to be witness to it. My cheeks burned, and I prayed he wouldn't see me. He sucked in his breath, just as I had, at the sight of the bruise. He looked into her eyes and said, "Your hand, what about that? Is it broken?"

She shook her head, no.

"The bastard," Blue muttered his voice husky with hatred. "This is it, Mom. Do you understand? I will *not* --This is the end."

"Please," she whispered. "I *know*. Don't." She raised her good hand to his face and brushed her fingers down his cheek in a gesture so filled with love, I shivered. "Please," she said quietly, "just take me home."

"No," Blue said. "Not there, I mean it. But I will get you out of here." He put his hand on her shoulder, "Do you need help, getting dressed or anything?"

She must have responded, no, because I heard him crackling a plastic bag with her clothes in it, handing it to her, then zipping the hanging curtain around the bed to give her some privacy. He stepped out and leaned back against the wall. He propped his left foot up, his head sank, he sighed and he shut his eyes tight. He crossed his arms tightly across his chest, holding himself in. I held my breath and dreaded him seeing me. If he glanced up, I would be exposed. Though all I wanted was to get out of my bed, walk over and put my arms around him, to hold him. I knew then what Rusty meant by Blue having "family problems." How many times had this scene been repeated? The horror of it stunned me, silenced me. It was then he glanced up and saw me.

At first, it was like he didn't recognize me. Finally, his eyes seemed to focus and I felt that familiar heat spread all through my body, as it always did when those green eyes latched onto mine. He looked at me first with surprise, then wariness. He just stared at me and I could read the hard words in his eyes. *Don't. Don't ask. Not now.*

I stared back, hoping he could see the sympathy in mine. I just nodded at him, swallowed hard, indicating I understood. He looked away then, staring into space, and after what seemed like a long time his mother called faintly, "Blue...."

He went back behind the curtain and I heard him helping her back into the chair, "Just stay in here until I get you out to the car...." he said.

So he wheeled her out and past my bed, his eyes meeting mine one last time. They were filled with anger and pain and my own eyes brimmed with tears. His mother just looked down at her hands. Then they were gone. There was only a pause of maybe three or four minutes, when my mother rushed in.

"Jamie? Honey?" she asked, peering into the room. Once she saw it was me, she rushed to the bed. "Oh, honey—are you all right?" Right behind her, the nurse finally came back with my water.

I reached for my mother and as she put her arms around me, I started to sob. Everything I had been holding in came out. And it wasn't even about the ache in my foot anymore. It was about Blue and his mother, and what I saw in both their eyes. Imagining what they had lived through. My mother just held me and stroked my hair and I felt so utterly, deeply grateful.

"I love you, Mom," I sobbed, "I'm so glad you're here. I love you."

"Oh honey, so am I. Thank God you're all right. I was so worried; Mrs. Morrisey called and told me what happened. It's all right now, we can go home. They said you were all right."

When I calmed down, we talked. I explained the whole foot incident, how it happened and what followed. But after what I had witnessed in the room next to me, my episode seemed far less monumental. I was going to be fine. The doctor said my toes would heal in a few weeks. I wouldn't be able do my lawns for a while. I had stitches and some deep cuts, but miraculously, I lost no toes and only my small toe had been broken. I was lucky. But Blue's mom...maybe her face would heal and her hand-- but her eyes. How could that look in her eyes ever go away? I couldn't stop thinking about them, and worrying. *Oh Blue*, I thought, *I wish I had known*. In that moment, I forgave him Patty, forgave him all of it. At least I was going home to a place that was safe.

CHAPTER TEN

The next two weeks dragged. I had to sit around waiting for my toes to heal, watching soaps and *Magnum PI* re-runs, reading, listening to records, and to Sally telling me many intimate and unwanted details about Walter Harvey on the phone. Every now and then, I'd go hobbling into the kitchen for iced tea or food. But never far from my thoughts was Blue. I had even been concocting schemes in my mind for getting information about him from Rusty. The problem was I couldn't tell anyone what I knew about his circumstances. I had promised him, with my eyes, if not my words. I couldn't stop worrying about what was happening to him and to his mother. Mom was endlessly patient with me groaning about how bored I was and how my precious summer was being wasted. I actually missed cutting my lawns. Luckily, I had only lost one of my customers while being laid up. Everyone else was understanding and said they would get temporary help until I was better. By the end of the second week, I had cabin fever.

I had begun to wander the house and the yard, in aimless circles, in my awkward heel-down limp. I had to keep my toes propped up off the ground, putting weight only on my heel, which made me look like a lopsided penguin, but at least I could get around a little that way. The bandages had gotten progressively smaller, until now I just had some adhesive tape holding a small gauze pad wrapped around the injured toes. My stitches were melting away. By next week, they said I could take it all off and begin walking more normally. My broken pinkie toe hurt the worst, and it was still black and blue and swollen.

Friday afternoon, I was alone. Mom had gone to the grocery store, and I was limping around the front yard when I heard the familiar whine of a motorcycle engine. I turned and saw the glint of silver chrome coming up the street. My heart thudded, but then I told myself it must be Rusty. Listening carefully, I knew that was a smaller engine than Rusty's 1100, and he was at work anyway. I squinted and let my head fall sideways, trying to see in the glare of bright sunlight what color it was. I wasn't sure, but it was coming closer. My mouth went dry.

The motorcycle paused at the intersection and then eased forward slowly toward our house. *Okay,* I told myself, *stay calm. It's probably not him.* I went and sat down in a battered lawn chair, watching, waiting, acting like I didn't care. It was black, yes, I could tell now, it was black all right. It was inching along, as if looking for something. Maybe he was making sure I wasn't my mother. I couldn't believe it-- it had to be Blue. Could he actually be looking for *me?* I wiped a trickle of sweat at my temple. I had on old jean shorts and a stupid white Harley tank top, but it was too late for changing now. In what seemed an eternity, the motorcycle pulled up to the curb in front of our house. And there he was, all that gold skin and long legs in faded jean cut-offs and a blue tee-shirt. I could feel his tension, idling there, and knew he was jumpy as a cat, ready to run. He wore no helmet and his blond hair shimmered around his head. He glowed, but his face was grim. He waved me over toward him nervously, glancing around as the bike engine idled quietly.

I tried to saunter toward him sultrily, or at least normally, but I was still listing to one side, I knew. I had to move slowly, acting like I was not about to faint at all, which I was. He looked gold and as beautiful as ever. He slipped his gold wire-rimmed sunglasses off his face and looked hard at me.

"You okay, to go for a ride?" he asked, glancing down at my bandaged toes.

I nodded. Yes, *anything, anywhere,* I thought, *take me away.* "Only for a while though. My mom's going to be back soon."

He nodded back, his face serious, and handed me the blue helmet I wore on our first ride, while he thrust his sunglasses back on. I prayed my mother wouldn't get back before I did. She would panic. But I could tell Blue wanted something, having to do with the day at the hospital and his mother, I was guessing. So I climbed on behind him, and we zipped off down the street with the chrome glinting in the mid-day sun and the bike warm between my thighs. I pulled my arms around Blue's now familiar waist, my hands clasped one over the other in front.

He drove for ten minutes or so, through several intersections and traffic lights, and I enjoyed every minute of the feel of him, his firm back, his smell, his hair blowing against my cheek. He finally pulled up at a small seafood restaurant with a deck outside, overlooking a creek. We parked, slipped off, and Blue said, "C'mon, out here…." I followed him up a small wooden flight of stairs to the back deck, and since it was the lull between lunch and dinner, there were only a handful of other people there. Brown pelicans sat on some old pilings below and the harbor was flat and deep jade green. Blue chose a table far out toward the corner, overlooking the water, where we could be alone.

He gestured for me to sit and he did too. Once seated, he removed his glasses and tossed them onto the table in front of him. We were shaded by a green awning that stuck out of the building overhead. He looked into my eyes and then down at the scarred wooden tabletop, silent. He began to light a cigarette from the pack he pulled from his pocket, the gestures now familiar to me as well. I drank him in like water and admired his hands. I showed no signs of impatience, though I was dying for him to get talking. But I said nothing, sensing he needed time, to do this his own way, at his own pace. He was so easily pushed away. I had to be careful with him, patient.

The waitress came over and we both ordered cokes and nothing else. She didn't look happy about that, but said nothing. Once she left, Blue took a big breath and began haltingly, "I know what you saw the other day--at the hospital, must have got you wondering." He stopped again. Swallowed, took a drag. "I just wanted to explain some stuff so you wouldn't be talking--to your friends or…whoever." He looked away, out to the water.

"I wouldn't do that," I said. "I'm not like that."

"Well, I just wanted you to understand…" He went on, waving his hand for me to stop and closed his eyes. "This is, not the first time my mother has been there, like that. Not the first time, for damn sure," he said disgustedly, shaking his head and looking down. "My stepfather has a little problem, you could say. He drinks. He hits. Look, he's a bastard. I hate him." He looked up into my eyes with that, the green glittering and hard as glass. "My mother can't seem to stay the hell away from him. Every time she just says he didn't mean it, or it's not that bad, or it's only when he drinks, or he promised he'll stop…Blah, blah. Once or twice, she even packed a bag and I almost had her out of there. But he's good. He'll convince her it's all over, that he loves her. He's got all the right words. But it never stops. Maybe for awhile, he'll be 'good.' He'll swear he won't drink anymore, and for months at a time, it's okay. But then, slowly, his engine starts running hot again, he starts getting eaten up inside by his own poison, and everything she does starts to bug him, and I feel it coming.

"For the longest time, I *know* it's coming, I smell it. And for the last two years, he only does it when I'm not around, because I told him if he hurt her again, I'd kill him. I meant it and he knows it. I'm big enough to really do it. It's why I haven't left this damn town since I graduated.

69

I just--can't leave her alone with him. I would really love to hit him, you know? Just once, punch his face in real good. It would feel great, after watching what he's done to my mother for the last twelve years. But I haven't yet, because I--" He gulped in some air and looked into my eyes again, with the same desperation "-- I don't want to be him, *become* what he is. But I do want him dead, don't get me wrong. I want him *gone*."

My heart ached as he spoke, for all that he had been through. For the anguish there was in his house, the scenes he must have stored in his head, and for the scars, inside and out, the wounds inflicted on them both. Nothing he could do to stop it. I could picture Blue at six or seven, thin and blond, silent, seeing or hearing the fists falling, the thumps, groans and stifled cries. Not knowing what to do. His mother the next morning, moving around the kitchen like she was old, broken. No wonder Blue hung out at the beach with his friends where they partied, I thought. No wonder his music was so full of pain and light and dark, so haunting. No wonder he had to keep more than one girl going at a time, so no one would get too close or know too much. It all became clear, it all made such perfect sense. Yet here he was, confiding in *me*. It sent a silent shiver through me, because it was a huge honor, but also, a huge responsibility…to know.

"But I, can't-- do it anymore. I am so close." His eyes were staring out at the water, but not seeing it, seeing those old scenes in his head. "I am so close now that I'm afraid I really will--kill him." His voice was hard, dead-sounding. It scared me too. I believed him. He went on, "I have got to get her out of there, or I have to get out of here." He looked hard at my eyes again, his filled with that dark searing pain I had seen in the hospital. "She's at my apartment now, but she won't stay. I know it. She's not talking, just sitting and staring out the window all day. He keeps calling, begging for 'One more chance.' Right, one more, one more *millionth* chance. I told him to stop calling, to shut up, leave her alone, but I can feel her slipping back. She doesn't even believe she can make it on her own anymore; he's done that to her. He's never even let her work, since we moved here. He's made her feel that helpless. That worthless." He stopped again, trying to collect himself. He drummed his fingers hard on the table, rattling the sunglasses. The waitress smacked down our cokes and walked away.

He looked down for a long minute. Finally, he looked up at me again, his eyes lightening for a moment. "I think I told you, my mother used to be an artist. She taught me all about the greats; remember I told you about Picasso? She showed me paintings in books and took me to museums. Before my dad left---she had some shows even, in galleries, back when we lived in California. She was known there, Caroline, the artist. I always remember her drawing and painting. She was good. But when I was three, my dad just left. I hardly remember him. He used to make good money, cross-country trucking, but he left to join some second-rate rock band, touring, and never came back. Since they were never officially married, he left her high and dry. She had to work two jobs then. She stopped her art, she hasn't painted since…"

"I don't think he's ever even tried to contact her, or bothered to find out anything about me." I could hear the pain and wonder in his voice, that his father could do that. "He's probably got some other family by now."

"We were trying to get along on Mom's teacher salary, not doing too good, when my Mom met *Don*. He seemed great, at the beginning anyway. He treated her nice, had money, was always buying us presents and flowers, fixing things around our house, and acting nice to me, too. But it was all just a huge pathetic joke--what an act. Ha. What did I know? I was just a fricking kid. Once she married him, it started. Not too often at first, but slowly, it got to be more and more regular. He screamed, told me how stupid I was and all that crap, but he never did come out and hit me. I think he knew if he did, she'd leave. But she just stopped being herself."

"She used to be…full of light, and laughing all the time. Once they got married, he convinced her to quit her job. She may have stopped painting, but she still loved teaching art to those kids. She taught little kids. He cut her off from everyone. Over time, she got quieter and more far away and I just--couldn't bring her back. I couldn't get her *out*." His voice was thick with guilt and anguish.

"So," he cleared his throat, "here we are…twelve fricking years later. We moved to Florida cause he opened a car dealership here. This was supposed to be a fresh start. Yeah, right. No one would ever know, cause he's Mr. Perfect, *right? Mr. I'll give you a deal.* Everybody in town thinks he's *great*." His words, filled with disgust, drifted off. Then he looked back into my face. "Look, I don't know why I'm telling you all this. I don't talk about this, with *anybody. Ever*. But you saw, and I just felt like, I needed to explain. Just don't blab this around."

I reached over very slowly and covered his hand with mine, carefully, so as not to startle or scare him away. He looked into my eyes and for the first time that day, the slightest flicker of a smile turned up one corner of the hard line of his mouth and his eyes softened.

71

I could tell he wanted to change the subject. "What the hell did you do to your toes, anyway?" he asked, the slight line curving up, almost into a grin.

"I tried mowing the grass with them," I replied, glancing down at my bandaged toes, wanting to seem brave and even more, to make him laugh. "But they weren't sharp enough."

And he laughed one big burst of belly laughter. That made me feel so light and giddy, that I started giggling too, picturing my bare toes buzzing through the grass like a set of clippers. "Foot clippers," I said. "They're the latest thing…" And before I knew it, we were both snorting and guffawing, about nothing really, just needing to laugh. The waitress gave us a dirty look. But we couldn't stop until our stomachs ached and we were gasping and tears started running down both our cheeks. It was such a relief, and so much easier than crying.

CHAPTER ELEVEN

Only minutes after Blue zipped off, as I was limping across the lawn, my mother drove up. Another narrow escape, I was afraid I might be running out of those.

"Hey, Mom!" I called cheerfully, trying to cover my guilt as she climbed out of the car. "Want me to help carry some bags in?"

She swung open the trunk and looked at me skeptically, "You aren't even supposed to be walking around this much, J. I think you better get back on the couch. Next week, hon, they said you could start to do more. You're almost there." She picked up one of the bags and carried it toward the kitchen. I groaned and limped back to my prison term on the couch. *Three more days*, I told myself, but at least now I had another memory of Blue to turn over like a smooth precious stone in my mind. I smiled when I thought of the two of us laughing at the outside picnic table, but it faded quickly when I thought of his mother. Then I realized that once more, Blue had ridden off without a clue as to when I might see or hear from him again.

*   *   *

I was walking around almost normally a week and a half later and was back into my summer work routine, though I was newly respectful around the lawn mower, as if it might turn on me any minute. I still couldn't shake Blue from my mind and, of course, there had been no word from him. Every time the phone rang, I'd fly up to answer it first, hoping. It made me crazy, angry, confused. Why tell me his most important secret and then retreat behind his wall of silence again? I found myself scheming up ways to see him, while my better side told me to stay away. The worry that he was probably spending time with Patti boiled often in the pit of my belly, but I wanted to keep some semblance of my pride. He was going to have to reach out for me this time. If there was going to be a next time.

It was mid-summer now and the heat was bearing down like a truck on the highway. These were the days when all I'd do was drip. Even the inside walls of the house were sometimes coated in a thin film of sweat and mildew could flower on the bathroom tiles overnight. The three air conditioning units we owned-- two in the bedrooms, one in the family room--were always on, their thrumming our constant background music.

Outside, the air was thick day and night. At mid-day, I could almost feel it swirl in waves around me as I moved. The cicadas droned endlessly from the trees. This was the time of summer I dreaded out cutting lawns, the bugs, the heat. At least each afternoon a thunderstorm would move in out of nowhere, pelting down huge fat raindrops so thick it made cars stop on the road, blinded. Then the sun would break back out like it never happened and the heat would return. When I came home my clothes were plastered to me, a heavy second skin. The only cure was a long cold shower.

Sally was wrapped up in Walter Harvey and though she called, I didn't see her as much as usual. Surprisingly, I had even kept Blue's secret from her; that was how loyal I was to my promise. I had other friends who called occasionally and who I went to get ice cream with, to the movies or the beach, but part of my mind was always on Blue. Always wondering where he was and if he was okay. I knew my mother noticed I was preoccupied, but thankfully, she hadn't confronted me about it. Not yet anyway. She was watching me, though, I could tell.

One Saturday night while Mom and I were finishing the dinner dishes, Sally called and invited me to a party at a senior's house, a friend of Walter's. Sheer boredom compelled me to say yes. Mom agreed, as long as I was home by eleven, so Sally said she would pick me up at 8:30, on her way, because she was meeting Walter there.

I was happy to see Sally's familiar blonde head inside the Go-go as she squealed up to the curb. She was grinning broadly and hollered out the open passenger window to me, "Whoops! Hope your mom didn't hear that!" She had the Allman Brothers cranking out of her speakers. "Long time, no see!"

"You're crazy!" I yelled back, sliding into the seat next to her. I turned the volume knob down a notch, so that at least we could hear each other speak without screaming. "How could she not hear you? One of these days, Sal, you're gonna get nailed, Mom's gonna see the real you. So, you are actually meeting Walter there…all on my account?" Sally smirked at me. "So where's this party?"

"Very funny, but *yes*, I wanted it to be just us girls, for a change. This guy Ted's house! He's cute, maybe you'll like him. I think he just broke up with Jeannie Blakeman. You know, he's the basketball player, tall, with light brown hair?"

"Yeah, I know who he is," I replied, but picturing him gave me no thrill, no rush of heat through my body. Sally must have read my mind, which she had been known to do.

"So what's up with that Blue guy anyway? Have you seen him lately?"

"Yeah, once or twice."

Sally slammed on the brakes, swerved, and almost bounced off the car in the right lane next to us. "*GOD*, Sal!" I yelled. " *--Watch out!*"

"YOU HAVE?" she screeched at me. "Why didn't you tell me?"

"I don't know," I answered, "it's not like he's calling me all the time and we're having this hot, heavy thing or anything." I *wish,* I thought to myself. "I've just run into him a few times, that's all."

Sally glanced over, her eyes narrowed, and said, "*Run* into him, huh? *Right.* You aren't telling me everything, Jamie Monaco…you are NOT telling me it all. And what exactly *did* happen that night at the fireworks? You never said."

I really didn't want to go into that night. It seemed like ancient history and it only made me worry that he might be with Patti right that minute. Then it hit me: Patti was a senior. What if she ended up there, at the party, with Blue? "Nothing," I replied, my stomach tightening. "Don't worry about it. So tell me more about this party, who's going to be there?" I knew it would work to change the subject. Sally loved to talk about all the seniors; I knew she thought it was cool that she was hanging out with them now. So for the rest of the ride, she fed me all the intimate details of their love lives, family life, likes and dislikes, who was cool and who wasn't. Sally had amazing memory for people trivia, though none of it really stuck in my head. All I was thinking about was what I would do if confronted with the nightmare of Blue and Patti there, together, which now seemed a likely scenario. Sally drove out to the Key. As we rode over the bridge span, we looked down at the Gulf, a layer of rippling jade beneath us.

We finally turned into a winding crushed-shell driveway. The party was at one of those huge beach houses tucked back off the road, the ones I admired and rode past that day on the back of Blue's bike.

"So, what's this guy's name, Ted what?" I said loudly, over the Allman Brothers and the hot air whooshing in the open windows. "His parents rich or something?"

"Definitely, this place is *cool*. Ted Fordham. Are you kidding, on the Key, right on the beach? You'll love it. Course, it will probably be a mess by the end of this party," Sally shouted back. "I don't think his parents even know about it. They're away some place—and millions of kids are coming--"

"Great," I replied, thinking, *just what I need, to be at an illegal party where a rich senior's house might get totaled, and where I also may be forced to observe Blue and Patti, up close and together.* Well, at least I'd finally get to see the inside of one of those beach houses -- but it was slim consolation. In fact, I felt queasy. Sally skidded, then parallel parked the car in an open spot along the driveway. There were cars lining both sides of the narrow road, which made it impossible to try to approach the house.

"C'mon," Sally said swinging open the car door, then slamming it, "time to party."

I got out too and we started up the drive toward the house. After walking around a bend, I looked up and whistled low. "Wow," I murmured. The house was a huge peach stucco, wood and glass construction that reflected the setting sun. It had a huge double wood front doors with long wrought iron handles Behind it lay the Gulf, reflecting the colors of the sunset and the white sand beach. On the right side of the house we could see a spacious lanai, lit up and sparkling with strings of white lights, with a huge pool in the middle of it. Aerosmith was blaring into the night. Kids were jumping in and out of the pool and were scattered all over the house. We could see them through every lit window.

We wandered in a screen door and started wading across the crowded kitchen. Sally immediately spotted Walter getting a beer from the fridge and squealed. She ran across the room, bumping off bodies as she went, and threw herself into his arms. Now I figured I would be *alone* and confronted with Blue and Patti. But after Sally hugged and kissed Walter a few times, she turned and waved me over. I reluctantly waded through the crowd too, wishing I had stayed home. The senior I had been in the baseball dug-out with the night of the fireworks recognized me and shouted, "Hey, look, it's Slugger." I curled my lip, sneered at him and moved on. Sally handed me a can of beer, Walter said hi, and they went back to kissing again.

I glanced into the dining room and saw a group of guys in baseball caps playing poker around the dining room table. No one seemed to notice as I wandered uncomfortably from there to the living room, which was littered with seniors and their friends drinking, passing joints, and

76

laughing loudly. I put the beer down on a counter, pretending to accidentally lose it. I had enough of drinking on the Fourth of July.

The sweet scent of pot was also thick in the air. Bodies were dancing in the dim living room light, and the whole first floor was vibrating with the stomping of feet. There were wet rings left by beer cans and overflowing ashtrays on almost every available expensive wood surface, including the dining room table. Kids were sprawled across couches and making out in corners. *Oh no*, I thought. *The house.* The beautiful mahogany bar in the living room was covered with bottles and kids were helping themselves to the booze. There were kids everywhere you looked, and half of them I didn't even recognize, older kids, not even from our school. Some of them looked like the rough crowd that hung out at Blue's beach parties, and that worried me. I peered around anxiously, afraid of seeing Patti and Blue nuzzling on a couch or in a corner. I couldn't breathe. I turned and hurried out to the lanai, at least there I could feel the breeze and get some air.

It was crowded there too, with kids splashing each other and diving, getting in and out of the large kidney-shaped pool. I imagined how it must look without so many idiotic people jumping in and out of it, peaceful and serene. I drifted out the screen door to walk the beach. I didn't belong at that party any more than I did at the one I went to with Blue. I guessed I wasn't much of a party person. But take me to a place where Blue was playing, to a cool dark bar where I wasn't even old enough to drink, let me sit at a table in the back carried off by the sound, and there inside the music, I could be free.

The beach too had always made me feel at home. I slipped off my sandals to feel the cool sand under the bare soles of my feet. The Gulf was calm and glassy in the rising moonlight, lapping softly onto the beach. I breathed deep, glad to be outside, alone and strolling along the water. I walked slowly for a few minutes, shuffling my feet, and then I heard voices ahead of me in the gathering dusk. I recognized one of them immediately and it stopped me dead: Blue. The higher, shriller voice, I knew too.

"God, you're wasted. *Stop* it. I *mean* it."

"C'mon Patti," Blue's voice was thick and slurry. "You know I love you."

His words cut through my body like shears through a scrap of metal, leaving jagged edges, *you know I love you*. I strained to see where the voices were coming from, to make out the shapes of their bodies, but though the moon was just rising on the lip of the horizon, the dusk was blue ink by now, hard to see through. I wanted to run, get away, not hear any more, but I was paralyzed.

"*Blue, quit* it! I'm sick of this!" And suddenly Patti was rushing toward me, her midriff-baring white tank top floating like a ghost in the dim light, so I backed away from the edge of the water where she was walking, hoping she wouldn't notice I was there. Lucky for me, she was whisking along through the sand with her arms pumping fast, head down, long hair swinging. She blew past me and I caught a whiff of her heavy too-sweet perfume, the scent of roses. I breathed out only when she was a small white blur going toward the lights of the house, and thought, now *he's out here, alone.*

"Patti!" he called after her, his voice anguished, thick. "Dammit, Patti!" But no answer came. I moved cautiously toward his voice. I had to. He always pulled me in like this, his current too strong for me to swim against. I knew if I had any sense I would leave, get away, not humiliate myself any further, after having heard the words that kept bonging like church bells in my head, *you know I love you....* But I couldn't do it, couldn't leave him there alone. Even when I knew it wasn't me he loved.

So I moved toward the voice, until I saw his dark shape sitting in the sand, his elbows propped on his knees, head in hands. I didn't want to startle him, so very quietly, I said, "Blue?"

"Patti?" He looked up, confused by the sound of my voice.

"No...it's me, Blue, Jamie."

"*Lil' shister?* Sheezus, how'd you get here?" He sounded foggy, slurring his words.

"Well, I came to the party. You know the one down there," I gestured toward the house," with my friend Sally. Patti, uh, she went back there," I said, pointing toward the house. But he wasn't even looking at me. I sat down in the sand beside him, wanting to rub my hand down his back, to comfort him like my mother did when I was sick sometimes, but I didn't dare. As always, his nearness made me dizzy, and it was still hard for me not to touch him. Even though I could tell he was messed up and probably dangerous, I had to hold myself back.

Blue laughed, one short burst that didn't even sound like laughter, more like a sob, "Doesn't matter," he mumbled to himself. "Doesn't fricking matter."

I didn't want to ask what he meant, but hoped it was that Patti's being gone didn't matter. I knew he probably meant everything. "Blue?" I asked, "You ok?"

Again, the thick snort of laughter, "Oh, yeah, jus' had a little too much...to drink. *Jamie, Liddle sister...*" his voice changed with the last words, becoming soft and whispery. The way he said my name sent a shiver through me. "Can I, Can I jus..." and his face looked up toward mine and even in the dark, I could see the pleading in his eyes, the desperation. His hand brushed down my cheek clumsily. He pulled me toward him and crushed me to his chest, holding onto me with all his weight. I could barely breathe. I almost said, *too tight, Blue, too tight.* But then I heard a sound escape him, a terrible rasping breath, then another, almost a groan, and I realized he was crying. His whole body was racked with it, shaking. I got my arms around him somehow and held on, finally rubbing my hand down his back in long strokes. "It's okay," I mumbled. "It's going to be okay," and he sobbed in my arms, his body going heavy and limp. My chest ached and I felt a thickness in the back of my own throat.

And then his words came out in jagged breaths, "She went back— she—Ga-damn--- she--went back," and I knew he meant his mother, not Patti. His mother went back.

I didn't know what I could say or do that would make any difference. I felt the weight of it myself, just holding him in my arms, picturing his mother's hollow eyes and bruised cheek. He pulled back from me as abruptly as he had grabbed on, and punched his fist furiously into the sand. "I *told* you! I told you she would---I fricking KNEW it!" He punched again and again, his fist leaving a deepening dent, sand flying everywhere. I was afraid in his drunken state he would hurt himself, his beautiful hands. I wanted to reach over and grab them, to still him, but his hot fury intimidated me. I was afraid he might even lash out blindly at me.

What could I say? That maybe this time it would be different? That she would be all right? Should I tell him that he should do something, take her someplace far away, out of his reach, when she kept going back? What could I say that would change anything? Suddenly, I felt too young and too old at the same time. Blue's predicament too dark and unwieldy for me to handle. But I couldn't walk away from him. I had somehow gotten tangled up in his life, and though maybe he didn't yet realize it, I knew he needed me.

Then his mood shifted again. He looked over at me in silence and pulled me toward him, grabbing my shoulders so hard I thought he was going to shove me backwards. But then he pulled me in, his lips covered mine and he kissed me hard, almost biting. He kissed me and kissed me

79

and though I was as lost and dizzy as I always was when he touched me, there was something scary and out of control about it. He pushed me down hard into the sand and covered me with his body. I felt the whole length of him against me. He was heavy and strong, pinning me to the sand, his legs straddling mine, kissing too hard and going too fast, as if he were drowning and I was a raft he was clinging to. He pressed my hands down flat beside my head, his palms heavy over mine, our fingers entwined. My body heated, I couldn't help responding to him, wanting him-- but he was scaring me too. *Please*, I thought, *not like this.*

"Blue," I said firmly. "Blue, *Wait*." But he didn't even seem to hear me. He kept kissing me, hard and long, his tongue probing my mouth. I could barely breathe. I tried to push him off. In his drunken state, he was like dead weight. I couldn't budge him. "Blue, STOP!" I ordered. "*Stop* it!"

Finally, my voice seemed to penetrate, to get through to him. He pulled his mouth off mine and looked down into my face, his eyes focusing, suddenly realizing what he was doing. I saw surprise and shame flicker across his features. He lifted off me fast and though it was a tremendous relief, there was also something wrenching about letting his body separate from mine too, letting him go.

"Oh God," he mumbled. "God, I'm—sorry. Sorry."

I sat up and brushed some of the sand off me and he mimicked my movements, gently brushing the sand from my hair. "I'm okay," I said. But the power of him, his need and ferocity, had shaken and confused me. A heated desire all mixed up with fear of him was racing through my bloodstream. Rusty sure had been right about the bomb ticking, Blue was that all right.

"Blue, I-- we need to walk..." I said, suddenly knowing it was the right move. "Let's get up and take a walk." I scrambled up and held out my hand. He grabbed onto it and got up unsteadily. "C'mon," I said, "this way." We set off along the water's edge, away from the party, Blue taking big crooked strides, not walking quite straight. He leaned on me, heavily, for balance. I took most his weight with his arm looped across my shoulders and tried to keep him steady, gripping tight to the belt loop at the back of his jeans. He was too heavy for me, but I did the best I could to steady him as he strode clumsily along, his hip bumping beside me. I remembered a song my mother taught me as we walked in playful zigzags down the beach with our arms wrapped around each other's shoulders, singing. *We...are...a little bit... crazy*...we'd sing, and then bow toward the sand at the end, *one, two, three, four...we are a little bit crazy*. Then start the whole silly zigzag walk again.

"You're the only one who knows," he said, quietly. "The only one."

His words sent a shudder of longing through me; I wanted so much for it to be true. Yet I also wanted to confront him—*but what about Patti, you said you loved her.* He was drunk, so how much of any of it did he mean? About any of it, being able to talk to me or loving Patti--how could I know what was real?

He stopped and turned sideways, his gaze fell down to my face and he cupped my chin in his hands. He started to kiss me again, but this time it started out soft and gentle, his eyes open, looking down into mine. His lips knowing how to caress mine sip and taste them. Then he grew more insistent, hungrier, parting my lips with his tongue and leaning his body against mine, his hands running all over me. I never knew a kiss could have so many tendrils, could pull you in so deep you could get lost in it. His touch vibrated all through me. I kissed him back and it got harder and harder to stop. And I didn't want to, but I knew he was drunk, and what would it mean to him later? Would he even remember? A low moan escaped Blue's lips, "Baby," he murmured, "oh, Jamie."

"Blue," I murmured back, "I...we should get back." He was capable of confusing me so completely; I lost my direction, my center. It was scary to feel you could disappear into somebody, until their pain and need could become your own. I had always been so strong, no one pulling me off my own headstrong course. Until now.

"Back where?" he mumbled, "Can't we jus stay...sleep here, in the sand?" He twisted my hair gently in his fingers, making me dizzy with longing.

"No," I murmured. "I mean, I can't. I can't be late getting home."

"Oh," Blue's voice was again thick with sadness. His fingers tugged my hair, pulling, then dropped away. "'Kay, well, you go, then. I'll stay." He started to sink to the sand.

"No!" I jumped to catch him, to stop him from sinking down. It would be too hard to get him back up and moving again. "I mean, I think you should come with me. We should both go back to the party."

"No," he said gruffly, sitting down hard. "You just go--go on back."

"I can't do that, Blue. I don't want--did you come on your bike?"

He wouldn't answer me.

"You rode your motorcycle, right?" I tried again. I could see a slight nod. "Okay, well, you can't ride that right now."

"Look, I take care of *myself,* got it? Just g'on back. You're a--kid anyway, jus a gaddamn kid, *leave me* alone," he grumbled.

81

His words burned down like a searing metal tip into wood, and I knew he was too drunk to know what he was saying, and also that he was trying to hurt me. It hurt anyway, and I almost did just walk away right then, just give up on him. He was so exhausting. But I couldn't. It didn't matter to anyone except me if Blue slept on the beach, because no one was waiting for him to get home, with his mother too tangled in her own nightmare. I imagined it had been like that a lot for him, for most of his life.

"Blue, I have a car," I said, my thoughts racing. "I can take you home so you can leave your motorcycle here until tomorrow. Okay? C'mon, let's both go back."

I could feel him hesitate. "Please?" I asked, and offered him my hand again. I hoped I could somehow get him to cooperate, though how I was going to get Sally to agree to drive him home was another problem. He grabbed on and I pulled him up, but this time he didn't loop his arm across my shoulder or touch me at all. He just walked along beside me in silence, his steps long and still crooked.

I breathed deep, trying to slow down my thoughts and figure out what I was going to do next. How could I get him home without explaining everything to Sally? Blue wouldn't want anyone involved but me, that much I knew. As we got closer to the rectangular patches of light on the beach and heard the strains of music pulsing, I sensed Blue's tension. The house seemed huge in front of us, intimidating.

"I'm heading out," he muttered. He started to stride off toward the front of the house where I was sure his motorcycle was parked.

"No," I sputtered, "I mean—wait a minute! I'm going to give you a ride, okay? I'll just run inside to tell my friend I'm leaving, just one minute. You can wait by the car. It's right down there, the blue Volvo sedan around the bend, on the left. It's unlocked! " I called and dashed toward the house to find Sally, hoping he would, *please* stay, until I got back. My heart was tripping hard, my breathing ragged; I wondered how in the world I was going to convince Sally to hand over the keys when she knew I'd be driving her father's car illegally--or if I even wanted her to. But things were moving too fast and I saw no other choice. It might mean saving Blue's life, but I wouldn't tell her that part.

I dashed into the house and finally found Sally in the living room with her arms around Walter's neck, dancing to the Beatles, "Golden Slumbers." *Boy, you're gonna carry that weight, a long time...*

"Sally," I tapped her frantically on the back. "Sally, please."

She turned around to face me, surprise on her face. "Oh, Jamie? What?" She could tell immediately from the expression on my face that this was serious.

"I need the car keys, Sal. Can't explain now. You're just going to have to trust me on this, please. I'll be right back, just for a half hour or so, okay?"

"Jamie, I don't know. What's this about? You're acting so weird lately."

"Sally, please, I can't talk about it now, but it's important. Just give me the keys."

She looked at me skeptically and shook her blonde head. "I know I'm going to regret this," she mumbled, as she went over to a closet where she'd hidden her India-print bag. "Your mother is going to kill me...and *you.*" She shooed a couple people out of the way and started pawing through the bag. I went over and stood beside her as she rattled on. "I swear to God, Jamie, if you crack up that car, we are both DEAD. Do you read me? Do NOT let ANYTHING happen to that car. You've got to promise - over your scrawny little body - NOTHING will happen." She dug out the bag and uncovered the keys, handing them to me reluctantly.

I looked her and said, "I swear, Sal, I swear, thank you," while silently pleading for her to hurry up. I grabbed the keys and hugged her quickly, saying, "Don't worry," and then started weaving across the room, darting through the crowd. "Don't you make me sorry!" Sally called after me.

I had to get back to Blue before he got into trouble, or hopped on his bike. I pushed as quickly as I could through the people and rushed back outside. I ran all the way down the drive to the car. As I rounded the bend, I couldn't see Blue anywhere. *Dammit.* I panicked and called, "Blue? Hey, Blue! Where are you?"

"Here," I heard a faint reply. I glanced around but couldn't find him, then looked inside the car. He was stretched out on the passenger side, the seat tilted to recline. His head was back, his eyes closed, his legs stretched out as far as they could go. "He's right here," he mumbled.

Thank God, I thought, and quickly opened the driver-side door. *Okay, now all I have to do is drive--illegally.* I tried not to think of my mother, or my brother. I carefully put the keys in the ignition, grateful that at least Blue wasn't watching me. I put my shaky hands on the wheel and took a deep breath. I clicked on the key and listened as the engine turned over. *Okay,* I thought, *lights...release the brake, you can do this...*It was tricky that the car was parallel parked. I hoped I wouldn't hit anything. *Please*, I thought, *I can do this*...I put the car in drive, nudged it forward, and tried to peer over the hood to see how close I was getting to the car ahead, but it was hard it was so dark. I stepped on the brake, stopped, and took another deep breath before backing up a little and cranking the wheel. I felt the car bump against the car behind me. *Oh God, Oh no.*

It roused Blue from his half-sleep, and he slid the car seat upright. "D'you hit something?"

"Nah, it's fine," I replied nonchalantly. "Just a tap." Okay, I decided, I would have to look at it later. I nudged forward again, but didn't seem any closer to getting out of that damned spot. I backed up again. I jumped out and checked the bumper I'd hit. Whew. Couldn't see any damage. I slid back in behind the wheel.

Blue laughed. "Jeez, Lil' Sister, you drive much?"

"All the time," I replied. "I'm just--*new* at it." I concentrated on easing back slow, not hitting the bumper behind me again. I refused to look over at him, now that I knew he was watching. I slipped the car into park, giving myself a rest. Then, finally, I nudged forward again. I was only a few inches closer to getting out. One more time back, then forward. Blue laughed again and said, "This is good, I think I need a joint to get through this," and started pulling a folded baggie out of his front pocket. He fumbled around with the bag and pulled out a crumpled up rolling paper. *No, no*, I thought, *I can't deal with this too.* Finally, I prayed that I had enough room and took a wild lunge at pulling out. Miraculously, it worked. We just barely cleared the front car's bumper. The problem now was that we were facing toward house, not out, and I doubted I had room to drive up the driveway to turn around. Cars were parked everywhere.

Blue had somehow deftly rolled the joint and was about to light it with the cigarette lighter. I said quietly, "Blue, this is somebody else's car. I borrowed it. And if it smells like pot when I bring it back, well, I'm dead. Sorry, but could you...maybe, *not*, right now?"

He looked over at me, the joint dangling from his lip. His eyes were still cloudy and dazed looking, but he seemed to see my point. He removed the joint and grinned over at me, "Thought you said it was your car."

"Yeah, I know," I admitted, "I lied."

"You wanted ta give me a ride home that bad?" he asked.

"Well, yeah, I guess so," I answered.

"Wow. Lil' sister, you truly do never cease to amaze," he said, the s's of his words slurry and thick. "Never do cease. But the drivin' needs work."

I laughed at that. I couldn't help it. I never expected his sense of humor to return over my shoddy driving skills. "I know. But I can do it well enough to get you home."

"*Bye-bye, motorcycle, bye-bye, motor bike -*" Blue sang, to the tune of *Bye-Bye Love*, waving to his motorcycle out the open window, as I slowly and shakily backed the car down the long driveway. Blue whooped if I veered too close to a car or the bushes, and with his help, I made it all the way down, though I still couldn't believe I was actually doing it. Now I just had to get him home and me back in one piece. "All right, Little Sister! Knew you could!" he shouted, when we hit the open road.

Once we were out of the long drive and on easier terrain, my body relaxed. There weren't many cars on the road and I eased up to forty-five, concentrating on not swerving too close to the middle line or the white edge line. I knew my eleven o'clock curfew must be coming up fast. I had to drop Blue off, get the car back without the cops stopping me, and get Sally to take me home by then, all of which seemed impossible. But at that moment, I felt flush with the victory of getting the car free and keeping Blue off his motorcycle. The fireflies and stars were blended together, white sparks flickering in the blackness around us, then gone.

The night was fluid around us, our car windows open to it. Blue put his head back and closed his eyes. He began to sing. His voice flowed out low and thick at first, then grew stronger and clearer, slipped like a drug into my blood, and became my pulse. I remembered the ride on Blue's bike to the beach, how close to him I'd felt, a connection beyond words. And I still was high with him beside me now, as broken as he was. I was lifted up on his voice and everything was worth it. Just to be there while he sang into the night wind for me alone. It was one I'd never heard, a new one, so filled with pain and longing, my throat got a lump while I listened. It was a country-tinged ballad, slow and keening:

Leaving sometimes
Is the only road left
Closing the door
On the blows and regrets

When you have grown old and weary
Of the secrets and the games
Of the four more last chances
'Cause you know he won't change...

So she's trading her pain
For the freedom and rain
Not going back
Never going back
For more...

The song for his mother, clearly, a plea for her release. His words were moving like water inside me and I wanted to keep him there, to hold him close and safe in my soul. I hardly dared breathe as he sang, because I was so afraid I would break the spell and he would drift away from me again. He was so good at disappearing.

When we finally pulled up to the apartment house Blue directed me to, I didn't want to leave him. We hadn't spoken since he stopped singing, but the power of it still hung there in the air between us. "It's beautiful, Blue," I said, wishing the words he sang were true.

He said, "It's not finished yet."

If Taraberg had a bad section, Blue lived in it. The two-story apartment house sagged visibly in the one bare streetlight out front. It had a stained stucco exterior, once white, but now yellowed. The yard was a few prickly wisps of grass clinging to a bed of sand, with a broken-down fence out front. He sat with his arm propped out the open window.

"Home sweet home," he muttered. Then, without warning, he turned and cupped my face in his warm hands, and stared at me with an unreadable expression in his eyes. He kissed me hard and fast, and pulled back before I could catch my breath. He started to pull himself out after he swung open the car door, still a bit unsteady.

"Blue," I called, wanting one more word, to make it all better, something, I didn't even know what-- just wanting.

"You better go now, Little Sister," he said gently. "Thanks for the ride." He walked away from the car, his steps drifting slightly left, then right, but finally making his way to the entrance. I watched as he squeaked open the screen door and took a key from his pocket. Only one light was on in an upstairs window. He fumbled with the key for a few seconds, then got the door open. He lifted his hand over his shoulder in a kind of backward wave, but didn't turn around. "Bye," I called softly, knowing he was already gone.

CHAPTER TWELVE

After that, everything happened so fast. I was driving back to the party carefully, under the speed limit even, worrying about Blue. Something in his mood when I left him had me scared. I had the oddest sensation that I would never see him again. I left the windows open to the warm night air, hurrying to get the car safely back to Sally, so I could get home. I had no idea what time it was but knew it must be close to midnight. Way past my curfew.

I was on the last stretch of road to the party only five minutes away, feeling confident I had pulled it off, when out of nowhere, I saw blue lights flash on in the dark behind me and heard the harsh *Brr--RRRRR—* of the siren. I was nabbed. My whole body surged with adrenaline. *No, I* thought, *Oh no...my mother. Rusty's going to kill me...Sally.* I slowly and shakily pulled the car over to the sand strip on the side of the road. Yep, it was me he wanted, because the cruiser pulled in right behind me.

The blue lights flashed so harshly and so close behind my bumper, I had to squint to keep from being blinded. The sirens sent my heart into overdrive. I felt like it was going to pound right through the skin of my chest. The cop approached my side door with his flashlight waving ahead of him like a long antennae. He leaned down, peering in, shining the flashlight into my face, "License and registration," he demanded. I couldn't see his face at all, just the huge black rim of his hat. I wanted to cry, but I was too scared.

Not knowing what to, I fumbled around in the glove compartment and by some miracle, I grabbed onto the registration in a clear plastic envelope. "Well, here it is," I said, as friendly as I could. He shined the light right in my face as I handed it to him. "It's not my car," I stammered on, "it's my friend Sally's. I borrowed it for just a minute, to take a friend home."

"License," he demanded. My heart hammered even louder.

"Sir, I don't—" What could I say? Make up a big lie about leaving it at home and then get found out later? My Dad always said, *just tell the truth, Jamie, 'cause the little lies just keep on growing.* "Sir, I don't have my license just yet."

"Please step out of the vehicle," he ordered, with the pulsing of the lights getting more and more on my nerves. With the flashlight on my face too, I thought, *How many lights does this guy need?* I was talking to a robot, not a person. I could tell he was trying to tell if I was stoned, or drunk.

I wasn't sure my legs would hold as I opened the door, with shaking hands, and slid slowly up to a stand. He shined the light from my face and then all down my body. "How old are you, Miss?"

"Sixteen," I replied. "I was planning on getting my license this fall," and realized I kept rambling on unnecessarily.

"You do realize driving without a license is a crime." He said it as a statement, not a question. He shined the light right in my eyes, looking into my pupils. "Is this a stolen vehicle?"

"No! Oh, no!" I retorted, panicked, wincing in the light. "My friend Sally loaned it to me, like I said, to take a friend home." I didn't add, *a friend who had too much to drink.* My mind raced to what was going to happen when he asked me where I had come from, and then everyone at the party would get busted too. I had really gotten myself into it this time.

"Where can this *friend* be located?" he asked. Why did cops always ask everything in technical jargon, like they were speaking a different language?

"Ummn, she's at another friend's house, not far from here." I was totally rattled. "But can you, uhm, just wait here, maybe, and I'll go get her?" I knew I was making a total fool of myself and that Mr. Robot would never let me do that, but I was just desperate for a way out. I couldn't lead him back to that party, with all the drinking and pot smoking. The whole school would despise me. But if I kept babbling on stupidly, he was going to think I was high on something.

He swept the flashlight off my face to the ground and squinted hard at me. "No, Miss, that's *not* possible."

"Well, maybe you just better call my mother, then," I replied. "Maybe that would be easier."

"Does your mother know where you are?" he inquired, his voice loud and barking.

"Yes," I said hesitantly, "she knows I'm with Sally, my friend." Oh God, this was getting worse and worse. I was probably going to spend the night in jail, at the very least, and then my big brother and Sally were both going to kill me once I got out. My mother was going to disown me. I was throwing my life away. I pictured my mug shot, with my dreams of college disappearing before my eyes.

He looked at me hard again, and then said, "Please follow me." He led me to the cruiser and opened the back door. He shielded my head as I got in, like I was a raving idiot who was going to bang it heedlessly on the roof. The wire screen that separated the back from the front seat made me feel like a dog in a kennel. He snapped the door shut and walked around to the driver's side door. He reached in his open window and grabbed his radio from the dash, stretching the cord back outside to talk. He was mumbling something about a "minor... driving without a license." Then he paused, looked at me and said, "Name."

"Oh, Jamie Monaco, I live on Five Jacaranda Drive."

He said my name into the radio too, and something about bringing me into the station for questioning, then something about calling my mother. *Okay*, I thought, *I can deal with this*. It wasn't good, but it was better than getting everyone at the party arrested too. I could imagine what Sally's parents were going to say when they found out about the car. They'd probably think I was the one who was a bad influence on Sally, not the other way around, and never let me see her again. I felt a thickness in my chest and tears welling up in my eyes. The cop went to Sally's car, placing one flare behind it, and one in front of it. Then he ambled back and squeezed into the driver's seat, saying not one word to me. He drove me to the station in complete silence. I guess he figured the best way to terrify the "minor" into submission was to say nothing. It was working.

The drive to the station was unbearably long, and I was scared and exhausted. I felt like I had been through three nights of this never-ending saga, instead of one, with no sleep. I didn't dare rest my head back on the seat, thinking of all the greasy criminals and derelicts that had been there. I wished the cop had a police dog, at least then I'd have some company-- that is, if it didn't bite my head off.

I knew I had this coming. All summer, I had been taking huge risks, breaking rules with abandon, being in the *Apple*, drinking, sneaking out, lying to my mother and now driving without a license. It all led me here, and I knew I deserved it. I wasn't a bad kid, I was just letting a guy I was crazy about lead me into trouble, time and time again. I'd always heard love made you stupid. Now I knew it first-hand. But I was... in love. I had to admit that to myself. Why else would I risk all this? Even riding in the back seat of a police car, something I could never imagine happening to me, and I still couldn't say Blue hadn't been worth it.

That was when I heard it. It came scratchy and broken-up over the police scanner. Some numbers, a woman's voice, "Domestic situation, that's a 10-61 in progress at Buena Vista 913--" static interrupted the rest. The police officer asked for a callback. She read the address again, mentioned the need for backup and an ambulance. The officer replied that he had to make a "minor drop-off," and then would assist. All at once, I understood why the address sounded so familiar—it was Blue's mother's house.

*   *   *

My mother stood pale and strained, her mouth set in a hard line, waiting for me in the police station lobby. Rusty was another matter. Scowling darkly from the minute he saw me coming down the hall from the holding room, I knew I was in for it. But I was too exhausted and worried to care. Mom came right to me, taking me into her arms. I hugged her back gratefully and said, "Mom, Oh, Mom, I'm so sorry. I'm such an idiot, an idiot. I was only trying to help."

She held me for a long time, rocking me side-to-side, like I was a five-year old, and it was just what I needed, such a relief to be safe, to be loved. "Thank God you're all right, Thank God," she murmured. Rusty stood with his massive arms crossed on his chest, glowering at me. His eyes saying, *Yes, you are an idiot,* and *I will deal with you later.*

"And Blue?" I asked, looking up at him. "What happened?"

Rusty looked confused at first, then he made the connection. "What do you mean, what about Blue?"

"I heard it on the police radio, on the way here; there was something bad happening, at his mother's house."

Rusty looked at me as if to say, and what would *you* know about that? But he could see there was something desperate in my eyes. "I'll go ask," was all he said, worry reflected in his expression now too, and I wondered what he knew. He hurried off to the front desk.

Mom looked from one of us to the other, "What's all this about, Jamie?"

"I've got a lot of explaining to do, Mom. And I know I should have told you about this before, but I couldn't, I kind of promised, and it's all just too hard to go into now. I will, I'll tell you *all* of it-- but right now, I've just got to know if Blue's okay."

"You do," she nodded, looking more angry than relieved, now that she could see I was all right, "have a lot to explain. And you'll be lucky if I ever let you out of the house again. My God, Jamie, a call from the *police*. Do you have any idea what that did to me? To both of us?" What she didn't say was, just like the call from the hospital, when Dad died. Her voice was hushed but tense. "To say nothing of Sally's family. They're furious. Whose idea was it to go to that senior party anyway?"

I didn't want to say, *Sally's*. Besides, my mother would never believe me, given the circumstances and the other lies I had told, the truth didn't sound very convincing. So instead, I shrugged.

"Never again," she shook her head and looked at the floor, thoroughly disappointed with me, I could tell. If only she understood that I had just been trying to help, to save Blue's life and that I hadn't even liked the party, which was all stupid Sally's idea in the first place. I just didn't have the energy to explain all that. I was preoccupied with vividly recalling Blue's words, *I'm so close now...I'm afraid I really will...it would feel so good...after what he's done to her.* Please, I prayed, let them be okay. I stared after Rusty, wishing him back with news.

We waited for a couple of minutes, me nervously running my hands through my hair and pacing around. Finally, we saw Rusty striding back down the hall. His eyes looked dark and I knew the news wasn't good. *Please*, I thought, *let him be all right.*

"What, Rusty, *What-*" I called, as he got closer.

He shook his head. "They wouldn't tell me much. It just happened. But they took his stepfather away in an ambulance. That much I know."

I didn't really care about Don. In fact, some part of me was glad he got hurt. "What about Blue?" I asked. "His mom?"

Rusty shook his head. "Not sure. They didn't say."

"But, you think they're all right?" I pleaded.

"I think so, sounded like it. Why are you so interested?" Rusty suddenly turned on me.

"We're, friends," I said. "I--know him."

"Really," Rusty said sarcastically. "You *know* him, huh? So it's true what someone said, about seeing you at one of those biker parties on the beach, you were there with *him*, huh? My little sister...What else have you been doing, J? Didn't I tell you to *stay away from him*?" Rusty shook a finger in my face, bombarding, shooting his angry words at me like darts, with Mom watching.

"That's *enough*," Mom interrupted firmly. "*Enough* for one night. Let's all get home and get some rest. We'll find out more tomorrow, Jamie. For now, it sounds like they're all right. Come on, both of you."

91

I was never so glad to leave a place in my life, and I never wanted to go back. I prayed Blue wouldn't be going there either, to that stale smelling holding room in the back, or worse, to one of the dank cells Robot man had marched me past, on purpose, I was sure. How would I ever see Blue again, now that Rusty and my mother knew? Maybe my premonition of never seeing him again would come true. How would I find out what happened, if he was really all right? I couldn't get my mind around it anymore. I so needed to sleep.

CHAPTER THIRTEEN

Still groggy, I slipped from of my sheets and looked out the window. It was late morning, and I knew Mom had let me sleep in. The events of the night before came rushing back, filling me with fear and dread all over again and I bolted downstairs.

"Mom!" I called. "Mom! Where are you?"

"Here, Jamie," she called, from the garden outside. The midday sunlight was harsh and blinding. She was weeding her flowerbed. "What is it-- Are you all right?" she asked, looking at me worriedly.

I squinted, saying, "I--" I didn't know how to explain it all in a big rush, but knew I needed to start somewhere. "I need to call Blue, Mom. I just have to know --"

"Hold on, hold on, a minute, Jamie, not so fast. I think we better go inside first, and talk about this."

"--I'm scared, Mom. I really need--"

"I understand that, but I need to know more about what's been going on with you. Obviously, there's a lot you haven't been telling me. I had a feeling something was very wrong with you lately…I wish I'd acted on it."

So I went into the lanai and sat down with a cup of tea and my mom, and I told her about how I'd met Blue. I explained how we'd become "friends," and about seeing his mother in the hospital that day. I told her almost everything, except the parts where I'd been sneaky and deceitful. It was such a relief to have someone else know. I told her that Blue wasn't what she thought, just this wild guy who was nothing but trouble. I told her how gifted he was and how he loved his mother so much, he was sacrificing his own future trying to protect her. I didn't tell her about Patti, and his smoking pot, and the other bad parts because what good would that do? And I knew there were bad parts, I wasn't kidding myself about those anymore. I guess I was still protecting her from certain things too.

My mother listened, while it all came tumbling out. Then she said, "I really wish you'd told me about all this before, Jamie. Maybe we could have done something. Maybe it wouldn't have gotten this far."

Then guilt washed over me. She was right. I contributed to whatever catastrophe happened last night in my own way, because I knew what was happening and I kept it a secret, to protect Blue. It was obvious that an explosion was coming. Yet if I had told someone, would it really have made any difference? Would my mother have done something to stop it? I wasn't sure. But I realized that sometimes the difference between right and wrong got complicated by the people you loved.

"And also," my mother went on, "I'm disappointed that you didn't feel you could tell me. Though I have to admit, I wouldn't have encouraged it, honey. He's just not-- right for you at this age. You're too young to have to get involved in situations like this."

I couldn't say, *but I love him, Mom.* Because try as she might to be supportive and understanding, I knew my mother was never going to approve of Blue and me. She couldn't understand how I'd risk so much for someone like him. We were different in that way, she and I. I had never felt it more sharply and it made me sad. I loved her, but I could never *be* her.

"Anyway, I will let you call him. I know how much it means to you. But seeing him, Jamie? I think we better not push it. Not after everything that's happened. Let's just give this some time, okay? "

I nodded, thinking, *never going to see him again.*

"So go ahead, call," she said.

"Thanks, Mom," I said, getting up to use the phone in the hall.

"Jamie?" she called after me.

"Yeah?"

"I love you...you know that, right?"

"I do, Mom. Love you too."

*   *   *

I looked up the number in the phone book and called his mother's house, but got no answer. I tried again, nothing. I thought for a moment of calling Rusty and asking for his help. But recalling the anger in his eyes the night before, I decided against it. The only other option was Sally. I needed to call her anyway, to apologize, and to see if her parents would still allow me to speak to her. With all the people she knew, maybe there was something she could do.

94

"Sally?"

"Ohmigod, Jamie. You are SO lucky I'm the one that answered the phone." She was speaking fast in a whispered voice, and I was deeply relieved she was still my friend. "Are you all right? What in the *hell* happened last night? I've been dying to call you, but my parents wouldn't let me."

I told her how sorry I was, about the car, about everything. I said I was driving carefully and still didn't know why they pulled me over. Then I relayed the events of my night with the police, how I tried not to let them get to her and everyone else at the party. I'd told them I couldn't remember the address when they'd questioned me, so they'd called her parents to pick up the car instead. I explained how Blue had been drunk and I had to get him home.

"My God, Jamie," she uttered with amazement when she heard it all. "You're an outlaw, do you realize that? You are a wild woman outlaw! Man, that was gutsy! The party got broken up anyway. Ted's parents came home early. The house was trashed, the scene was *not good*. My parents are grounding me forever, probably, and they won't let me see you for a LONG time. Now you'll never be able to get your license this fall. Why didn't you just ask me to drive Blue home? It would have saved you getting your little self arrested!"

"I couldn't, Sal, he's just--not like that. He would have bolted for sure. But, there's more to it than that. I'm scared." Then I told her about the radio call and how there had been trouble at his mother's house right after I dropped Blue at his place. I said I had a very bad feeling when I left. I suspected he had gone over there, still drunk. I didn't give her all the details, but I did say that I knew his stepfather had a temper and that Blue had probably been part of a nasty confrontation. There was an ambulance called, I said, and I couldn't reach him at the house and somehow, I needed to find out what happened.

"Whoa, Jamie. Why didn't you tell me all this was going on?"

"I don't know. I didn't tell anybody. It seemed like nothing was happening really, and then something was, and Blue just, well, he doesn't confide in people, Sal. I think I'm the only one he ever has with, and I didn't want to ruin it. I guess I got in a little over my head."

"I guess!"

"And you were all wrapped up in Walter, and, well, it's hard to explain."

"I think I get it, J—most of it, anyway, and I guess I wasn't exactly there for you. I'm sorry for that. Look, I don't know what I can do.

My parents are watching me like a hawk. They *like* Walter, and I don't even know when they're going to let me see *him* again. Never mind *you*. I told them it was my idea to go to the party, by the way. But they are just *ripped* at me, at you, at the embarrassment of it all, more than anything, I think. It's going to take them awhile to cool off. But I'll make some calls, I'll see if I can help somehow. I don't even KNOW Blue. But maybe Walter will know something. I'll call you if I find anything out. Okay?"

"All right. Just don't say too much, you know? Don't blab it all around. But I can't stand sitting here doing nothing."

"I know, but for right now, I think you better. You've been in enough trouble lately. Maybe he'll call you."

"Not likely. He's so good at disappearing, Sal. That's the hard thing about him. And right now, I have this feeling he may be gone for good."

"What are you saying? He won't kill himself or anything, will he?"

"No, not that. I don't know *what* exactly, I just feel something, like he's slipping away." As soon as I said it, I knew it was true. Since I first met Blue, I felt such a deep connection with him, like no one I had ever known. It was this bond strung tight as wire between us, something unexplainable, beyond words. I could feel his presence all the time, even when he wasn't right next to me. Maybe that was why I thought I was the only one who could save him. But since he got out of the car last night, I felt like I was losing him, like he was drifting out of range to a place I couldn't reach. *Over,* I wanted to send out to the stars. *Please, Blue, come in, over.*

*   *   *

The day dragged on interminably and Sally called to say Walter hadn't heard anything. I was too edgy to sit still so I asked Mom if I could please just ride the three miles on my bike to *Hannan's Wheels*. I told her I needed get out of the house for a while and promised that tomorrow, I would get back to my lawn routine. She hesitated, but finally said yes on the condition that I return home in an hour and call from Rusty's when I got there. Obviously, I was on a short leash. I agreed, figuring if anyone would hear anything about Blue, it would be Rusty. Whether he would tell me or not was another story.

At least riding my bike gave me a chance to burn off some of my nerves and breathe in some air. The house felt too closed in. I rode as fast as I could, not even caring about the heat or facing the force of Rusty's wrath when I got there. It just felt good to move.

I parked my bike inside the garage and braced myself for the hard Rusty winds to come. I strolled over to peek into the office, no Rusty, just the fan whirring on high. I called Mom quickly, telling her I was there and would be home soon. I saw some tools spread out on the floor and a motorcycle with parts taken out of it, standing alone.

"Russ," I called, "you here?"

I looked all over the garage. No Rusty. So I went outside, thinking maybe he was out back. I peered around the side of the building, saw a black Harley parked there, and then walked around to the back. Rusty was with a friend of his I knew as Will. They were standing close, looking at the ground, talking. Will scratched at the dirt with the toe of his black boot. Rusty stood in his usual stance, listening, with his arms crossed on his chest. It didn't look like they were talking about business. So I wandered back to the front and sat on the front step, waiting for Rusty to get back, praying that it might be information about Blue.

It seemed to take forever. Finally, I heard the Harley engine turn over, rev a bit, then chug down the alley and pull out into the street. I held my breath. Rusty ambled slowly back toward the front of the shop, still looking at the ground.

"Hey, Russ," I said quietly, not wanting to startle him, or stir him up.

He looked up, saw me, and I got ready to get yelled at. But his eyes were filled with something else, not anger, but worry. He looked so much like Dad for a minute, I wanted to cry. "Hey, J."

"Did you—find something out?" I asked carefully, not wanting to pry or start trouble, but needing to know.

"Yeah," he replied slowly.

"What, Rusty, please."

He sat down on the step next to me and ran his hand back through his hair. He let out a breath and told me the story he heard from Will, who was a friend of his and of Blue's. The call must have come right after I left Blue at his apartment.

"Please," she said into the phone, "something's happened..." Blue didn't have his bike, so he must have run the two miles to the house in the dark. I could see him, running hard down the empty streets, fueled by the alcohol and anger still in his blood. His fear and fury building as he got closer, knowing this would be the last time, deciding that as he ran.

Pounding through the door, his eyes sweeping the scene, expecting the worst, as he had so many times before. His stepfather, staggering around, with his shirt off and belly bulging, his mother huddled on the couch clutching her arm, this time. Blue pushed past his stepfather, went to her, saying, "Mom, let me see." She couldn't even hold it out, it was bent so sharply from below the shoulder, a sickening angle, her face pasty, eyes dull with shock. Once he saw, Blue grabbed for the phone. Don trying to swipe him away from it, drunkenly, yelling, "Get the hell out of here, you piece of crap! Stay out of it, you little mother--" Blue turning, flailing blindly, pummeling him, in the face, in the chest and belly, hitting him anywhere his fists could land. Don leaning back, raising his hands up, but too drunk and slow, and Blue pounding and pounding, watching his stepfather's face turn pulpy. His mother crying in the background, "Please, stop." But Blue couldn't, it had been such a long time coming. Finally, his stepfather began whimpering as he slipped back, started to fall, clutching at his face, and then Blue heard the CRACK of his head hitting the edge of the thick coffee table, and blood pulsing from the split like red ink. A section of his scalp peeled back, spurting red. Blue left him lying there, went to his mother, picked up the phone.

Rusty said Don was still in intensive care, and his mother had a dislocated shoulder, but was otherwise all right. Depending on whether the stepfather pulled through, Blue might be brought up on charges. It was still unclear.

Rusty and I sat, side-by-side on the step after the story was done, silent, but closer than I'd felt to him in a long time.

"Did you know?" I finally asked him.

"I didn't know exactly," he said, "but I had a feeling. Blue never wanted us to come to his house. He always kept a distance."

"I knew too," I said. "I just didn't' know what to do."

"Man, Baby, you've given Mom some fits lately. You've gotta stop this running around behind her back. And you have to stay clear of Blue—this isn't up to you, anymore. You always think you can fix everything, J, but you *can't*. You can't fix this."

"I know," I replied.

"And if you cut it out, maybe I'll teach you how to ride a motorcycle this summer, for real."

I looked over at him and tried to smile. He draped his big arm around my shoulder. The weight of it felt good, safe. We sat like that on the step, for a long while.

*   *   *

CHAPTER FOURTEEN

A week and a half later, Mom brought me to the hospital for one final check-up on my injured toes. They were all healed by then, even the pinky toe was back to its normal color and shape. I could walk like it never happened, but they wanted to make sure.

Mom pulled into the parking lot and that's when I saw them, slowly making their way to their car, Blue's stepfather and his mother. It was Blue's mother, Caroline, that caught my eye first. She had a sling on her shoulder and her eyes were focused on the ground. She still had a beauty about her, her shiny dark hair, her delicate walk, but she had lost some of my sympathy. How could she let it just go on and on? Don was leaning heavily on her good side, shuffling along. It was he who was limping, he who looked the most broken. In the daylight he was just a weak, overweight old man, with shadows of black and blue still on his face, and a white bandage on the side of his balding head. So Blue had taken something from him after all, and that, I was glad for. She helped him into the car and my stomach clenched. Rusty was right, you couldn't save people, unless they wanted to save themselves.

"You okay, hon?" My mom looked over at me.

"Yeah… I'm okay. Let's go on in."

*   *   *

Three days before, I had been mowing my Tuesday lawns, as usual. It was hot, late in the day, and I was on my last job. The sun was slanting lower in the sky, and I noticed that the days were already growing shorter. Summer was nearly over.

I pushed the clackety mower toward the house and, wonder of wonders, Rusty came out to greet me across the lawn. Right away, I knew. But I tried to keep steady, to not let it show.

Rusty waited until I pushed the mower back into its place in the carport. We walked a few steps outside and stood looking at the sky. "Blue stopped by today," he said, not looking at me, just out, squinting.

I couldn't look at him either. I kept my eyes on the sun, dipping down behind a bank of clouds low on the horizon. I waited.

"He was all packed up. He sold his bike, bought a pick-up truck, can you believe that? Had all his guitars and his stuff in the back."

I nodded.

"He said he wanted me to give you this."

He handed me a postcard, with the night skyline of Nashville on it, buildings with lit windows against a black sky and bright stars twinkling above it. I turned it over.

Little Sister: Gone to look for the one you said was mine.

Love Always,

Blue

*   *   *

I tacked the postcard up over my bed and every night I imagined Blue playing on some stage in Nashville, where he belonged. I knew for me there wouldn't be another Blue. He had left a hole in me, and I knew some part of me would always feel it. I made up my mind that next time I fell in love, I wouldn't let myself get so lost along the way.

The rest of the summer I took Rusty's advice and stayed out of trouble. Slowly, Mom began to trust me again. I did learn how to ride a motorcycle and it was just as I imagined, like learning how to fly. Now I could fly on my own and didn't need anybody else to carry me, except there always seemed to be space where Blue should be, there next to me.

One day I was looking through some old photo albums of Dad, with pictures of Rusty and me when we were little. It made me ache the way time kept moving so fast and there was nothing I could do to hold it still. The current kept moving, taking people I loved away with it. So I dug out Dad's old Nikon 35 millimeter from the attic and started trying to freeze the moments that counted, to capture them the only way I could. Though pictures weren't the same as flesh and blood, they were real and something I could keep. I just wished I had one of Blue.

EPILOGUE

Summer 2000

Jamie let go of her five year old son's hand on the deck and said, "Go on out to the beach, honey, I'll be right there." Her eleven-year-old daughter was already there, with her husband Ted. Her mother was coming that afternoon to visit, as was Russ and his family, his wife Shelly and the two boys. The rental beach house had been a good idea, a great place for everyone to gather. Taraberg had become so built-up, it always made Jamie sad to see the new development each time she visited, but seeing the Gulf again still made her feel like she was home. Jamie and Ted could now afford to rent one of the beach houses she always admired as a kid. She wanted to load her dad's old camera before she went down, though she wondered why she was still taking pictures, on her vacation.

Her editor was supposed to call, with some final changes needed on the book she'd just finished. It was from a series she'd done on homeless children for a magazine, but it captivated her enough to evolve into a book, and this time she'd written the text too. She was supposed to call any minute, so Jamie decided to give her five. In her career, she had found herself drawn to people in trouble, especially children. Rusty had been right, she couldn't fix everything, but at least her lens could tell the truth. She wanted people to see, to know, about what happened to people like Blue.

The radio was tuned to the Tampa Bay station and while she was adjusting her camera, she heard the disc jockey say, "--A very special guest here today, a local guy gone big-time, dropping in for a chat and to play a few songs...." She reached over and turned the volume up, "So let's welcome, Blue Rider!" the DJ said brightly, and Jamie smiled. She couldn't believe it.

She had run into Blue not long ago, after all those years. She was catching a flight out of Boston, her new home, as he was coming in. At first, they just looked at each other, not quite believing, and then he scooped her up into his arms like she was still sixteen and murmured, "Little Sister. God, you look good." He looked the same, handsome and tan, though his hair was cut shorter, and he was wearing a diamond stud earring and expensive boots and clothes. She had read in a magazine that he had divorced not long ago. He had a son. They both had a few more lines. "You changed your name," Jamie said. "Mr. Blue Rider," and he smiled ruefully, "Yeah, well, that's what they do to you in Nashville."

They found a quiet corner in an airport bar and talked for half an hour, all the time they could spare. Long enough for Jamie to learn that two years after Blue left Taraberg, his mother finally left Don, when he died from a heart attack. Caroline moved back to California, where she still had some family, and began teaching art again. She never remarried. Jamie knew from the Taraberg grapevine that Blue had slowly worked his way up through the ranks of Nashville, first playing small clubs and dives, eventually touring the country, and finally getting his songs on movie soundtracks and radio stations. Jamie never lost the ache she got when she heard one of his songs on the radio, taking her back to that summer. She had been right, some part of her always missed him. There was a space for him inside. He told her about how hard the constant travel was, but also about the thrill of playing for thousands of people who knew the words to his songs.

As for herself, she told Blue she picked up a camera that same summer after he left, and never put it down. She finished high school, went to college in Boston, and there started her career. She told him she was married and had a daughter and a son. She said how much she wished she had pictures of him playing on the stage of the Apple that summer. "And guess what?" she'd said. "Rusty felt guilty after you left, I think, I mooned around so much, and finally taught me how to ride a motorcycle." He laughed and said, "Little sister, I never doubted you could. You saved me, didn't you?" They held each other a long time in the airport, before letting go...

The DJ on the radio was asking Blue about his past. Jamie still loved the sound of his voice, "Well, I grew up right around here, in Taraberg," he said. "I used to play at a club called the *Ripe Apple*, though it's gone now." Then the DJ asked him if he would play them one last song. Blue said, "Sure thing. Actually, this one is for a girl I used to know back then. Hey, Little Sister—just in case you're listening, you know that thing you did with the star? I think it worked...so this one's for Jamie."

> *Hot summer twilights*
> *Screen doors that squeak*
> *Sundown and fireflies*
> *The language we speak*

When the waves of the Gulf
Just kept rolling in
And the breeze heard our wishes
Kept our secrets and sins
I never will forget the taste
Of your skin...

But the time comes for moving
The sky fades to black

Change don't come easy
But you can't get it back
The summer, she's leaving
And there's no turning back
The Summer, she's leaving
And there's no looking back....

"*Mom!*" Jamie was jolted to the present when she heard her son's call from the beach. "*Come on!*"

"Coming!" Jamie answered. She stood looking at the radio after the last chords faded and she could no longer hear his voice. His words shimmered in the quiet of the kitchen. Her hand reached out slowly, and then clicked the power off. She stood still for a moment. Finally, she wiped her cheeks clean, picked up her camera and walked out through the screen door to her son.